Dear Romance Reader,

Welcome to a world of breathtaking passion and never-ending romance.

Welcome to ***Precious Gem Romances.***

It is our pleasure to present *Precious Gem Romances,* a wonderful new line of romance books by some of America's best-loved authors. Let these thrilling historical and contemporary romances sweep you away to far-off times and places in stories that will dazzle your senses and melt your heart.

Sparkling with joy, laughter, and love, each *Precious Gem Romance* glows with all the passion and excitement you expect from the very best in romance. Offered at a great affordable price, these books are an irresistible value—and an essential addition to your romance collection. Tender love stories you will want to read again and again, *Precious Gem Romances* are books you will treasure forever.

Look for fabulous new *Precious Gem Romances* each month—available only at Wal★Mart.

Kate Duffy
Editorial Director

YOU'RE THE ONE

Lynn McKay

Zebra Books
Kensington Publishing Corp.
http://www.zebrabooks.com

ZEBRA BOOKS are published by

Kensington Publishing Corp.
850 Third Avenue
New York, NY 10022

First Printing: October, 1999
10 9 8 7 6 5 4 3 2 1

Printed in the United States of America

For my parents, George and Willys McKay.
Are you enjoying this, Daddy?

And for a dear friend, Betsy Hogan, who keeps my life during the work week sane and well organized.

Prologue

March, 1984
Cocoa Beach, Florida

Stephanie Jane Powell stared at the door of Room 221 at the Three Palms Motor Court.

Room 221 was Dusty Derrick's room. It was after midnight, but she'd had to wait for her parents to fall asleep so she could slip out of the room. All their fault. Dusty had invited her to tour Cocoa Beach with him after dinner, but her parents had nixed the idea. They'd said that Dusty was only being polite. Polite? Couldn't they see Dusty really wanted to be alone with her?

He'd finally made the first move. He loved her. She knew it. And she loved him. Now it was up to her to show him she was ready for a mature relationship.

A laughing couple emerged from the room next door and stared at her curiously. In a panic, she tried the doorknob. Unlocked. He must have been expecting her.

Inside, she leaned against the door, surprised by the almost absolute darkness. She saw the glowing red numbers of the digital clock on the nightstand next to the bed. The bed. A sliver of pale moonlight outlined the naked body of the man sprawled across it. Naked. Stevie sucked in a breath and almost choked. He was so . . . male.

This was what she wanted, wasn't it? With shaking hands, she began to undress.

Dusty breathed deeply. Great dream. Breasts . . . full, smooth. Hair . . . mmm . . . strawberries. Mouth . . . peppermint . . . delicious.

He ran his hand down a curved hip. She pushed it away. Playing coy. Soothing words, deep kisses, and she finally let him touch her where he wanted. Tight, so . . . tight. He used his mouth and hands until she writhed against him, making soft sounds of pleasure. Ready.

He finally opened his eyes, sure his dream lover would turn into a motel pillow. But below him in the darkness, he saw a cloud of dark hair and two gleaming eyes. A figment of his imagination caused by months of doing without? He shook his head and squinted. She moaned and pushed against him.

Real, she was real. And she wanted him. He plunged into her, his shout of dismay blending with her small cry of pain.

"Oh, no . . . you were a virgin!"

"Not anymore, Dusty." She pulled his mouth to hers.

Damn, she tasted great. What the hell? She was willing, he was able and he might as well finish what he'd started. Then she started to move and he gave up the effort to think.

When he finally eased away from her, he grunted his satisfaction. And he wasn't the only satisfied one. He'd really surpassed himself. She'd called his name as she'd clenched around him, held onto him with an impressive grip when tremors shook her. Now she cuddled against his side, one hand playing across his chest. After a long moment of listening to his thundering heart and remembering how to breathe, he finally found the energy to reach over and switch on the lamp beside the bed.

"Holy cow!" He leaped out of bed. "What the hell are *you* doing here?"

Stephanie Jane Powell smiled and fluttered her long black lashes. "I think that should be obvious."

Horrified, Dusty threw the bedspread over her, though the sight of her naked body flushed a rosy pink would stay with him for a long, long time. He stepped into his briefs and struggled to figure out how the hell this had happened.

Stephanie Jane Powell. This was a major league disaster. He rubbed his shoulder. He'd pitched today and strained his shoulder. Painkillers had knocked him out. He'd been dead to the world when she'd sneaked into his bed.

Not all of him had been dead. He'd managed to do the deed and then some. With Stevie. He cursed his lack of control.

"Dusty?" she whimpered.

Dusty pressed the heels of his hands against his burning eyes. This had to be a nightmare. He made himself look at the bed. No such luck.

"What the hell are you doing here, Stevie? In my bed?"

Tears welled up in her chocolate brown eyes and he looked away. She was just a kid. He swallowed, sure for a minute he was going to be sick.

"Dusty, please don't be mad. I . . . love you. I wanted to show you, to make love with you."

"Love?" Dusty stalked over to the bed to pull off the cover, the movement making his head swim. For a moment the sight of her perfect rose-tipped breasts stalled the air in his lungs.

"Oh, no, little girl. Don't fool yourself that what happened here was lovemaking."

Her swollen lower lip trembled and she tugged the bedspread up to her chin.

"Why are you being so mean? I thought you'd be happy to—"

"What? Have sex with you in my sleep?" Dusty ran his hands through his hair, then pulled a chair up to the side of the bed, not sure how long he could stand without passing out. Painkillers. Damn, he was woozy. He sat down and looked at her.

"Listen to me, Stevie. This is the dumbest, craziest thing you could have done. Even in the minors we have baseball groupies who keep their own kind of score card. You one of them?" She shook her head, or at least he thought she did. The damned room was a blur. He rubbed his eyes again. "We just had unprotected sex. Don't you know how dangerous that is?"

"You're an athlete. Healthy," she stammered.

"Never assume anything, sweetcakes." He saw a tear streak down her flushed cheek and relented. "All right, I *am* healthy. So all we have to worry about is . . ." Dusty jumped up and paced the worn brown carpet. "Damnation, Stevie, you got some crazy notion of having my baby?"

"No!" Her tears were really flowing now and he felt like a first-class bastard. But he *had* been minding his own business, sleeping soundly in his own bed when—

He pulled on a T-shirt, then stepped into a pair of jeans. The movement made the floor shift under him and he had to hold on to the back of the chair. "How old are you now, anyway? Fifteen? Sixteen?" His stomach twisted and he swallowed, hard.

"Eighteen." Her chin came up. "I graduate in May. Don't you remember?"

"Right now I can't remember my own name." Dusty saw a pile of clothes near the door, a brightly flowered shirt and matching shorts. He threw them at her. "Thanks for waiting 'til it was legal. Now get dressed and get the hell out of here."

"But, Dusty." Stevie snatched up the shirt and drew it over her head. "I had hoped . . . that is, you were so friendly this week. I thought you really liked me!" She wiggled into her shorts and flung back the covers.

Dusty watched her step into white sandals before she turned to stare at him, obviously desperate for a kind word. Hell's bells, of course he'd noticed her. What man wouldn't look at her and think about doing the wild thing? Tan legs about a mile long, a curvy figure. Lots of soft, dark hair, the kind a man could run his hands through. And now he knew it smelled like strawberries. He realized he was close to doing something really stupid, like pull her back into bed and try for a replay. No way, no how. Wrong time, wrong woman.

"You're Mike's little sister, Stevie. I've known you all your life. Why wouldn't I be nice to you? Hell, your dad was my first coach in Little League." Dusty rubbed his aching shoulder. His head was getting clearer, but so was his pain. "Oh, God, is your father going to come after me with a shotgun?"

Stevie flounced to the door, jerked it open, then turned to glare at him.

"Don't worry, Dusty. I'm not likely to brag to Daddy that I made a fool of myself over you. We go home to

Houston tomorrow and you won't ever have to see me again!"

"Just a minute, Stevie. You have to let me know if this night has consequences. Understand?" He strode over to grab her arm, forcing her to face him. Her cheeks were pink and her eyes full of tears.

"Relax. I won't try to trap you into something." She tried to jerk away. "Let go of me."

"Promise you'll let me know," Dusty said through clenched teeth. "You're not so grown up, but you're going to have to accept full responsibility for your little stunt tonight." Dusty shook her arm.

"Hey, you overgrown ape, I am so grown up. And you sure weren't complaining a few minutes ago." She looked down and Dusty let her go. "But you're right that what I did was stupid. I wasted my spring break on you! And almost asked you to my prom!" She turned with a sob.

Dusty almost reached for her, but decided to let her go. At the door, she turned to shoot him one more watery go-to-hell look.

"By the way, Dusty. Thanks for taking care of my virginity. It was getting to be a real drag!"

She strutted down the concrete walkway, her shapely rear decidedly in motion. Dusty realized his mouth was hanging open. When she reached a door near the end of the motel unit, he saw her mop at her face, her shoulders heaving.

Maybe he should have gone easier on her. But Stevie needed to be cured right now of any urges to sneak into a man's bed.

Dusty closed his door, then collapsed on the bed. Unprotected sex. Damnation. This was the night from hell. He'd relieved Stephanie Jane Powell of her virginity and broken her heart. A double header. He rolled over, his shoulder aching.

A crush. She'd get over it. Unless . . . if she did get pregnant, he couldn't imagine how they'd handle it. His best friend would hate him. Both families would—

Dusty groaned and reached for another pain pill, then crawled out of bed and pulled off his clothes. He'd already snapped off the light when he jumped out of bed again to firmly turn the deadbolt on the door and latch the safety chain. One virgin in his bed tonight was more than enough.

One

1999
Houston, Texas

"Hey, Stevie!" Tom MacIntyre's secretary grinned and took a bite out of a chocolate donut. "You're just in time for the excitement."

"Excitement? Donuts?" Stevie forced a smile. The funeral she'd attended this morning had her eyes red and her spirits low. No reason to rain on Joyce's parade, though. She tugged at her black linen jacket, trying to close it over her more than ample bosom. "I'd love one, but I'm still fighting off my usual five-pounds."

Joyce laughed and washed the bite down with a drink of soda. "Not donuts! Dusty Derrick."

Stevie's stomach dropped to her knees. Now? She had to see him now? When she looked like a cow? She started to reach for her lipstick, but stopped.

"The baseball player? Here to see the chief of detectives?"

"In the flesh. And oh, honey, is that flesh divine." Joyce rolled her eyes. "He was nice, too. Flirty. If I wasn't married . . ." Joyce sighed and took another bite of donut.

Stevie kept her smile firmly in place, impatient with

the panic that clawed at her gut. It had been fifteen years since she'd made a fool of herself over Dusty. The mere mention of his name wasn't enough to send her running out of her boss's office. She was a detective, for crying out loud. A pro at hiding her feelings no matter what happened. She sat on the corner of the desk with deliberate nonchalance.

"I guess Dusty sees a lot of Mac now that he's pitching for the Astros."

"Dusty? Do you know him?" Joyce leaned forward, then slapped the desk, nearly jumping out of her chair. "Of course you do. He and Mac and your brother, Mike, all grew up together. Oh my gosh!" She waved her donut in the air. "I want the scoop! Has he always been such a hunk? Did you ever . . . ?"

Stevie placed a hand on her chest and sighed dramatically. "I'm not one to kiss and tell, but just between us"—she leaned forward—"I have lusted after that man all my life."

"And here I thought you'd forgotten all about me."

Stevie froze. Oh, that voice, a bit deeper, but unmistakable. Joyce giggled as Stevie straightened and turned.

"Dusty!" She leaned against the desk. A hunk indeed. Unfair. Women deteriorated with age—added crow's feet, gained five pounds. But at thirty-nine Dusty had matured into over six feet of masculine perfection. Unfortunately.

He grinned, put his cup of coffee on a nearby filing cabinet and held out his arms. "Take me, I'm yours."

"Let me see if I still want you." Stevie looked him over, her gaze moving quickly over the bulge at the front of his khaki pants to the blue knit shirt that stretched across his broad shoulders. It was ridiculous, but she could still remember being held against that athletic body, kissing those firm lips, even though their encounter had been more than a decade ago.

When she finally looked at his face, his brilliant sapphire eyes were daring her to do something outrageous. A dare? Stevie moved into his arms and poked the dimple in his left cheek.

"I'm not sure what my boss will say, but what girl could resist?" His arms went around her, pulling her closer until her breasts were crushed against his chest. Damn her smart mouth.

She took a breath and wished she hadn't. The subtle aftershave he wore was one he'd hawked on television. Seductive by itself, when combined with Dusty's unique maleness, it became an aphrodisiac. Surely something that potent had to be illegal. She should whip out her badge, and tell him he was under arrest for seducing women with his aftershave.

She was losing it. Totally. She'd moved on since Dusty. But the man did seem to push all her buttons.

"Hey, Mac," Dusty called over his shoulder. "Can we use your office?"

He tightened his arms around her and Stevie felt the power that throwing a fast ball for twenty years had given him. Okay, so a struggle would be undignified. She fluttered her lashes when he looked down at her.

"Oh, Dusty," she cooed. "Let go of me before I grab something I know you're awfully proud of and—"

"Stevie!" Tom MacIntyre, Chief of Detectives, walked around them and opened his office door. "Stevie, you definitely need to move out of undercover work. You've obviously been playing a hooker too long."

"Not long enough, I'd say." Dusty laughed, letting her slide out of his arms. "Hookers say yes, not no."

"And I'm sure you'd know." Stevie stomped after her boss. "I need to talk to you, Mac. Should I come back later?"

"No," Mac said, his face unusually solemn as he settled behind his desk. "I'm glad you stopped by, Stevie. I want your opinion on a situation Dusty refuses to take seriously. Sit down and I'll fill you in."

"Come on, Mac. I've gotten a few phone calls, found some surprises, that's all." Dusty held a chair for Stevie, then sat down next to her. "I'm sorry now I ever mentioned it."

"Surprises that indicate unlimited access to your house."

"Really, Dusty? What are we talking about here? An overzealous fan?" Stevie turned to look at him. He was too close and smiling at her again. The man was just too good-looking. Too masculine. Too . . . everything. She finally pulled a thought out of her scrambled brain. "What kind of surprises?"

"Somebody came in and left me some notes. Cut up a picture. More a nuisance than anything else." Dusty looked less concerned than amused.

"A picture?"

"One with Madonna. My visitor shredded it."

Mac whistled. "You hear that, Stevie? Madonna. Dusty, you really play in the big leagues."

Stevie wished she had a notebook so she could bash the two grinning men over their thick heads with it. "We're getting off track here, gentlemen," she said sternly. "So what about this intruder?"

"Like you say, probably an overzealous fan. Don't worry, Stevie. My heart still belongs to you." Dusty grinned when Stevie gave him what she hoped was a quelling look. Nice that he could joke about it. She'd never found anything to laugh about in that terrible night she'd made such a fool of herself.

"Stevie's right. This is serious. This stalker's getting past your security system." Mac leaned back in his chair. "And she's obviously a mental case, destroying a picture of Madonna like that."

"I don't consider that a great loss. Madonna will send me another one if I ask." Dusty winked at Stevie. "Stuff like that keeps my publicist happy."

"Like your underwear ad?" Mac shook his head. "You've got some nerve, buddy, showin' your stuff like that. No wonder women are obsessing over you. Have you seen the ad, Stevie?"

"How could I miss it? For a while I couldn't open a magazine without seeing Dusty in all his glory." Stevie watched him wince and roll his left shoulder. Apparently every woman fantasized about a lover who looked as good in briefs as Dusty Derrick. Sales for the brand had skyrocketed. She'd spent way too much time studying the ad, remembering. . . .

"Damned embarrassing, but it bought me a nice condo in the Cayman Islands." Dusty leaned back. "It's a great place to spend the off-season. You guys ought to come visit me next winter. Bring the wife and kids, Mac. Stevie, you can bring a bikini." He grinned, his dimples punctuating his amusement.

"Can we get back on track here?" Stevie forced herself to maintain eye contact. "Obviously your fan doesn't want to share you with another woman. Did she damage any other property? Make any threats?"

Mac handed Stevie a plastic bag with a piece of pink notepaper inside. "This looks like a threat to me."

" 'Trash like this isn't good enough for you. Save yourself for *me*. Love, Bebe,' " Stevie read aloud.

"Sounds more like a threat to Madonna than Dusty. Any prints?"

Mac shook his head and tossed her another baggie. "No, and the paper is common discount store quality. Look at this one."

Stevie took the bag. This message was trimmed with pink flowers. " 'Your dog doesn't like me. Make him be nice. Bebe.' "

Dusty frowned. "Damn it, that one worries me. I figure I can take care of myself, but what if she hurts my dog?"

"So what are we, bodyguards for dogs?" Stevie stood up, her depressing morning and the stress of finally coming face to face with Dusty catching up with her. She wasn't sure how long she could just sit there, discussing his 'case' as if Dusty were just another victim, without bursting into tears.

"Mac, I'll make an appointment with Joyce to see you later in the week to discuss my promotion. Maybe you and Dusty can find a kennel for his pooch. I've got work to do."

"Sit down, Stevie. I do want your input and we'll discuss your promotion later." Mac frowned her back into her chair.

"I can't put Ranger in a kennel, he always goes into a decline, won't eat and howls all the time. I usually leave him with my folks when I'm on the road, but I don't want them to know about this little problem." Dusty took the note from Stevie, looked at it, then tossed it across the desk. "Damn it, Mac. It's bad enough someone's getting past my state-of-the-art alarm system but she's in there messing with my things and upsetting my dog."

"If we can catch her, there's a case for breaking and entering," Mac said thoughtfully. "I got a report from the security company here, Stevie. It would take a rocket scientist to bypass that system."

"A rocket scientist with a weakness for baseball heroes." Stevie saw Dusty cross his legs and realized her eyes were taking a sentimental journey over his belt buckle and below. She jumped up to look over Mac's shoulder. Security reports indicated no forced entries. She concentrated on scanning the papers, determined to ignore the insanity that made Dusty seem so incredibly attractive.

"I see police reports here. The men in blue are handling it, Mac. I'd say bringing in detectives at this point is an over-reaction. We've got a few real crimes to deal with in Houston, Dusty. Little things like homicide, drug dealers, rape."

"Back off, Stevie. Dusty mentioned this to me over dinner. I asked him to come by." Mac tapped the thick file. "There are dozens of letters like this, some of them indicating she's been close to Dusty. Close enough to do him harm if she thinks he doesn't appreciate her charms. We've seen this scenario turn ugly before." Mac rubbed a hand over his receding hairline. "Think, Stevie. Dusty is a local hero. If something happens to him, HPD will catch hell for it."

"Dusty's six-two, two-ten. The woman would have to be an Amazon to take him down."

"Why, Stevie, you've memorized my measurements. I'm touched." Dusty grinned and put a hand on his heart.

Mac thumped his desk. "Quit clowning, Dusty. And, Stevie, you know all the lady needs is a handgun. Dusty's a civilian. But you should know better." Mac looked thunderous. "And we don't know actually if we're dealing with a male or female."

"Oh, come on." Dusty jumped to his feet.

Mac looked Dusty up and down. "There's a price to pay for showing the world how you look in your underpants, bud."

"Humph!" Dusty paced to the window. "You have no idea how much control it takes to pose for one of those ads."

"Didn't look like you were in such great control to me." Stevie flushed when she realized Dusty had turned to grin at her.

"I'm glad to know you've studied it so closely." Dusty walked over and put an arm around her.

Stevie shrugged away and glared at him. "Obviously, Bebe has been studying it, too. You need to be careful, Dusty."

"What do you want me to do? Hire a bodyguard?" Dusty sprawled in a chair and ran a hand through his hair. Golden hair, cut short and sun-streaked. Stevie looked away, determined not to want him.

"Why not? It sounds like a good idea to me." She walked over and sat down next to him again. Good. She was calm, unfazed by the mere inches separating them. She almost smiled.

"I'd take a lot of ribbing from the guys on the team if I started walking around with some steroid-pumped muscleman by my side. Especially if it got out that my stalker was sending me love notes on pink paper."

"Don't be fooled by the sweet words and fancy paper. I've seen situations like this turn ugly in a hurry." Mac looked at Stevie. "Stevie, tell Dusty about the Regina Lampert case a couple of years ago. I'd hate to go through that again."

"God, yes." Brutal, horrifying memories made Stevie reach out and put a hand on Dusty's knee. Regina Lampert. What if Dusty's stalker was as crazy, as vindictive? Fear shuddered through her and she felt Dusty's warm hand cover hers.

"Damn, Stevie. You look like you've seen a ghost." Dusty turned her hand over and rubbed his thumb across her palm. She shivered then snatched back her hand, disgusted that she reacted to a simple touch. Simple? Nothing with Dusty was simple for her.

"Maybe I have. I'll tell you about it if you'll promise to listen seriously instead of acting like a compulsive flirt."

"Flirt? Was I flirting?" Dusty's eyes opened wide. "You put your hand on my leg."

"It was involuntary. I was just—"

"Would you two cut it out?" Mac interrupted, frowning. "Is there something I should know about? You two got something going?"

"No!" Stevie gave Dusty a warning look that must have given him pause.

"Not now, anyway." Dusty gave her an assessing look.

"We never—" Stevie muttered.

"Oh, yes, we did." Dusty smiled and ran a finger across her cheek.

"You looking to lose the use of your pitching hand?" Stevie snapped, baring her teeth.

"Stop it, both of you. This is serious. Stevie, you forget where we went this morning?" Mac loosened his tie. "A funeral, Dusty. For Stevie's partner. Killed in the line of duty. I deal in life and death here and so does Stevie. Neither of us plays a game for a living."

"Would you like me to get my frivolous self out of here?" Dusty scowled and stood up.

Mac rubbed his eyes and stared at his friend. "Just sit down, buddy. I know what you do has its own stresses. But trust me to know about this kind of thing. Let Stevie tell you about Regina Lampert. It may help you understand why I'm so worried about you." Mac met Dusty's gaze until he shrugged and sat back down.

"Tell me, Stevie, I'm all ears."

Stevie wanted to shake Dusty for his attitude. Mac's reminder had been a jolt back to reality for her. Standing at a graveside, burying another friend had been rough, more than rough. But Dusty was a civilian and the danger wasn't real to him. She took a breath and stared at him, willing him to really listen.

"Regina Lampert was tall, beautiful, and a regular on one of the morning TV shows. She had a lot of fans because she came across as smart and down-to-earth, not just a pretty face."

"Sounds like my kind of woman," Dusty said with a grin.

"Right." Irritated, Stevie went on. "One fan in particular kept calling her, sending her presents, even following her. Back then, there were no laws against stalking so we couldn't do much."

"So what happened?"

"Regina announced her move to New York. She'd been hired for a spot on a network show. Her fan became enraged. He followed her home from the studio and kidnapped her. He didn't kill her. Just used a box cutter on her face."

Dusty shut his eyes for a moment.

"Dusty, he disfigured her, then left her bleeding on the street. That's how Stevie got involved. She was undercover near the location where she was dropped." Mac shook his head.

"I will *never* forget it." Stevie kept her eyes on Dusty. For a moment she could hear the screams again. What if the person stalking Dusty was just as deranged? The thought made her queasy. "She was covered in blood, hysterical. We called an ambulance and I rode with her to the hospital, trying to calm her down."

"My God! What happened to her?"

Stevie cleared her throat. "She committed suicide as soon as she was released from the hospital."

Dusty ran a hand through his hair. "Damnation, if you were trying to scare me, you've done a good job."

"We want you to know how these things can turn ugly," Mac said quietly. "I'm trying to figure out how to keep you safe."

"Okay, maybe I do need some kind of help. If I beef up my home security or hire someone to watch the house . . ."

"Not good enough." Mac held up his hand. "You *do* need a bodyguard. Someone with you around the clock."

"Come on, Mac. I can take care of myself."

"I'm with Mac. You need help, professional help." Stevie sat back. This was good. She was in the groove now, ready to give him advice that might keep him from becoming just another victim. Victim. There went her stomach again. The thought of Dusty hurt or worse made her feel sick.

Mac stood up and walked around the desk. "You've got to do something. I'd like to give you one of my men, but with my budget . . ." He leaned against his desk. "Any ideas, Stevie?"

"Well, Dusty can afford to hire protection. And if he doesn't want a male bodyguard, how about a woman?"

"A female bodyguard?" Dusty jumped up and stared at them. "You're nuts. I've got an image to maintain."

"Heaven forbid your macho image should be tarnished." Stevie stood, toe to toe with him. "You think a woman can't handle the job? I'll have you know I handle much worse than your oversexed baseball groupies every day." Stevie felt her face flushing when his dimples flashed again.

"Stevie's right, Dusty." Mac rummaged in his desk drawer. "And I know just the right person." He pulled out a business card. "Lacy McMahon. She's a top-notch private investigator and I guarantee you won't mind being seen with her." He held out the card.

"Lacy . . ." Stevie snatched the card, her hand brushing Dusty's. A sudden flashback remembered that hand skimming her body, melting all her inhibitions. "No."

"What?"

Stevie realized both men were staring at her. Oh, God, she'd said it out loud.

"I . . . I mean Lacy is okay . . . for a PI. But we're talking Dusty here, Mac." Stevie couldn't meet Dusty's interested gaze. "Dusty was Mike's best friend. Maybe I should . . . you know, take care of this."

She finally forced herself to look at Dusty. He was grinning, of course, taking this all wrong. "I'm a professional, Dusty. Trained in surveillance, self-defense."

"This could work, Stevie," Mac said suddenly. "Your promotion doesn't go into effect until the first of the month. That would give you two weeks." He frowned. "You'd have to take personal leave. I'd like to give it to you officially but—"

"Wait a minute. Stephanie Jane, are you really volunteering to guard my body?" Dusty put an arm around her shoulders.

"Stop it! You've got to take this and me seriously." Stevie shook off his arm and walked over to the window, blinking rapidly, determined not to cry. It was just that her nerves were raw. Funerals, especially police funerals, brought back too many memories. This morning they'd buried Riley, her partner—who had died guarding her on a stakeout.

The parking lot seven stories down blurred as she fought for self-control. Easier said than done, especially when Dusty, the man who'd haunted her dreams for more years than she cared to admit, strolled in and seemed oblivious to the real danger here.

"Aw, hell, I'm sorry, sweetheart." Dusty came up beside her and touched her shoulder.

"Sweetheart? It's Detective Powell, Mr. Derrick, and I'm nobody's sweetheart at the moment. Quit treating this like some kind of joke." She turned and pierced Dusty with her coldest stare. "Your best friend, my brother Mike, didn't take danger seriously either. He ended up dead on the steps of this very building before his fortieth birthday. I won't lose another . . . friend."

Stevie stepped away from him. She couldn't think clearly. For a moment there she'd been about to say something really stupid. What would Dusty think if, after fifteen years, she blurted out some nonsense about caring what happened to him? Damn, she did care, entirely too much. But volunteer to guard him? She opened her mouth to retract her offer when Dusty moved close enough for her to feel the heat of his athletic body.

"Friend? Yeah, I guess we are friends. You've obviously turned into a professional who knows a lot more about catching bad guys than I want to. I'm touched you want to help me."

Stevie swayed toward him, toward the shelter of his broad chest and strong arms. She told herself she ought to back away, run like hell out of this office, but her legs wouldn't move.

She took a deep breath and squared her shoulders. She could do this. She was a professional. She had to take care of Dusty because Mike would have wanted it and she could cure herself of this ridiculous crush at the same time. Dusty was just a man like any other, sure to disappoint her in the long run. With a slight smile, she walked around Dusty to sit again. She *was* in control.

"All right then," Mac said, rubbing his hands together. "You'd better start today, Stevie."

"Probably so." She tried to sound nonchalant.

"But you can't let anyone know why you're hanging around me. I'd never live it down. You can be my new main squeeze."

Stevie scowled. "Save that stuff for your baseball groupies."

"Damn it, that was uncalled for!" Dusty roared.

Mac put his head in his hands and groaned. He looked up and glared at both of them. "Stevie, if you're going to do this, I think you'd better try for some objectivity."

Stevie's mouth snapped shut and Dusty chuckled.

"Dusty, you have to treat Stevie with the respect she deserves. She's doing you a big favor and at no small risk to herself. Stalkers, crazed fans, whatever we're dealing with here, are unpredictable. This is serious."

Stevie and Dusty stared at each other with narrowed eyes as Mac settled back in his chair. "You're going to spend a lot of time together and be seen together in public," he pointed out. "Smile, Stevie. Right now it looks like you want to smack him."

Two

"I *do* want to smack you." Stevie snapped her seat belt with a decisive movement.

"What's the matter? Regretting your offer already?" Dusty started his black Ferrari with a roar of the powerful engine. He held back a grin, figuring it would just add fuel to Stevie's fire. What luck. What he'd considered a minor, okay, a major annoyance had given him Stevie chained to his side.

He couldn't believe how she'd changed in fifteen years. In his mind she'd stayed eighteen. Too young. Now she was strong, sassy, with a mature beauty that stunned him. Shifting gears, he eased out of the parking lot.

"I really appreciate you sacrificing your vacation time for me. Does this mean you still care?"

"Care?" Her lips were tight, her face a thundercloud. "I can assure you my teenage crush is long gone."

"Now that's a shame." Dusty wanted to laugh at her if-looks-could-kill expression. She could probably do it, too, with all the self-defense she'd learned in police training. Hard to believe, though. She looked too . . . touchable. The best word he could come up with while steering a twelve-cylinder sports car through heavy traffic.

"It's obvious you're not taking me seriously." Stevie gripped the bucket seat when he turned a corner. "Maybe I should have let you hire a PI."

"Why didn't you?" Stevie wouldn't look at him and her cheeks were pink. "Well?"

"You heard Mac. You're a sports hero. The local police would look bad if someone hurt you. And you were Mike's best friend."

"Yes, I was." Dusty reached over and patted her knee. "Now admit it. You'd feel terrible if this turned ugly and you'd let Lacy Whosis handle it."

She lifted his hand and dropped it on the gearshift. "Quit pawing the bodyguard, Derrick."

"But with a body like that it's so tempting!" Dusty gave her an exaggerated leer.

"Would you keep your eyes on the road!" Stevie made a grab for the dashboard when he accelerated onto the freeway. "And slow down before you get a ticket!"

"I'm not speeding, at least not much." Dusty shifted into fifth gear and blended smoothly into the traffic. "Mac said you're being promoted out of the field. This may be your last chance to get up close and personal with a victim before you start shuffling those papers."

Stevie pursed her lips and stared at him. "Forget any notions of turning this into some kind of reunion, Dusty. I'm here to do a job. I can't afford to let you distract me."

"This *is* a reunion . . . of sorts. And I'm sure a professional like you can ignore distractions." Dusty pushed a button and soft jazz filled the sports car.

Distractions. Stevie looked out the car window. Yes, she was trained to ignore ordinary distractions. But these—bright blue eyes, the throb of music that made the close confines of the car seem intimate and that damned smell again, so seductive it should be a controlled substance. This was not starting well. She *had* to focus.

Stevie reached for the window control and soon had warm wind whipping her hair across her cheeks. Any woman would be finding it hard to concentrate right now. She took a deep breath, almost choking on the exhaust of the eighteen-wheeler they blew past.

"So we're going to your house?"

"Right. Then I've got a game tonight."

"The papers claim you make millions a year. I admit I'm curious about where you live. Am I going to see the ultimate bachelor pad?" Stevie made herself look at him. Okay, she could handle this. He wasn't that good-looking. Just healthy, tanned, toned, virile.

He glanced at her with a wry smile. "I earn those bucks. And there's no bachelor pad, just a nice home in the suburbs. I don't throw around money on high living anymore. I'm looking toward retirement, planning for the future."

"But I read—" Stevie shut her mouth. Next she'd be admitting she'd read every tabloid article she could on The Player With The Golden Arm. He'd often been on the front page in the years he'd played in California, partying with movie stars, living in Malibu.

"Don't believe everything you read." Dusty turned down the volume on the radio and glanced at her.

"What? You've never had an alien love child?" Stevie had to laugh at his expression.

"Sure, laugh. If you were a public property . . . okay, so I have a sports agent who gets me noticed. Name recognition means bigger bucks at the negotiating table, and more endorsements." Dusty maneuvered his car down a ramp and off the freeway.

"I'd say your agent is a genius." Stevie studied his classic profile. "From tabloid covers to those underwear ads, you were everywhere for a while."

"Yeah. I've told him to back off now that I'm home."

"Houston must seem pretty tame to you after Hollywood."

Dusty looked over and winked. "Oh, I don't know. There's something very comfortable about being back, surrounded by family, renewing friendships. Like slipping into old sneakers."

Stevie ran her window back up, sure her hair was a windblown fright. She bet his Hollywood ladies had always been perfect. Perfect hair. Perfect bodies. Damn those five pounds.

"So we're old sneakers to you. Thanks a lot." Yes, she was definitely going on a diet, starting today. Wait a minute. She didn't care what Dusty thought, did she? Unfortunately, when Dusty turned on the charm as he was doing now, it was hard not to mellow toward him. Those "dare me" blue eyes, those "touch me" dimples and she was itching to brush back the swath of golden hair that had tumbled over his forehead.

She'd married and divorced since her night with Dusty, but somehow, despite her denial, her schoolgirl crush had stayed alive long after it should have died of malnutrition. This was dangerous.

Dusty glanced over at her. "I love old sneakers. It feels good to be home, especially since my baseball career is almost over. I probably won't even finish this season, you know. My shoulder's giving me hell."

"I'm sorry." Stevie put her hand on his tanned arm.

"Me, too." A wry grin twisted his lips. "But I'm finally going to have to face facts. Mac's right, baseball is only a game, a game for young people."

"Oh, Dusty, I'm almost thirty-four. Forty isn't all that far away. Why, for a man it's prime time."

"Unless that man plays baseball." His tone was carefully neutral but Stevie could see the prospect of retiring really bothered him.

She touched his shoulder gently. "Does it hurt now?"

"Three surgeries to repair my rotator cuff, hundreds of hours of physical therapy and my fastball is getting harder to control all the time. Hell, yes, it hurts." Dusty reached over and squeezed her hand.

Stevie jerked her hand back in her lap, the sizzle of Dusty's touch jolting her. She'd always been a toucher, never thinking twice about it. She had to stop it because then Dusty felt free to touch her back. . . .

"You're really going to retire?"

"I'd like to break Nolan Ryan's record for strikeouts before I quit and I'm almost there. If the shoulder holds out, I can bow out on a nice high."

"What's after baseball?"

"I'm working on a few things. I've had some offers to do broadcasting." Dusty grinned at her. "Can you see me in one of those blazers, interviewing some rookie out to break my records?"

"Thinking about this makes me sad," Stevie admitted. "But, sure, you're perfect for television. Still public, though."

"I know." Dusty sighed. "If it weren't for a few overzealous fans, I wouldn't mind it. Wait till you see the bag of letters I've received from Bebe. Over a hundred."

"I'll have to look them over." Stevie noticed they had stopped in front of a black iron gate.

"So you can learn something?" Dusty grinned and reached up to hit a button on the remote control clipped onto his visor. The gate swung inward.

"Those letters are evidence, Dusty. I'll be looking for clues, nothing more."

"Too bad. With the right woman, Bebe's suggestions could be dynamite."

The right woman? Stevie hated the fact that the very suggestion of being right for Dusty made her heart beat faster. Time to get this back on track.

"You keep joking about Bebe, but breaking and entering is no joke. I'm here to keep anything worse from happening."

"Worse? If you really think this is going to get dangerous then maybe I should get a guy in here."

"I've spent the past ten years doing dangerous undercover work and I can handle anything that this Bebe throws at me."

He drove down a winding driveway, pushing the button again to close the gate behind them, then winked. "Undercover, huh? I'd like to see you as a hooker." At Stevie's snort, he laughed. "Okay. I admit I'm impressed. Mike said you were one of the best cops he knew." He frowned at the house.

"Damn it, I almost hate to go in there. What kind of surprises will there be this time?" Dusty stopped the car in front of a three-car garage. "I don't know how you do it. Just one stalker's got my gut in a knot. I can't imagine dealing with that kind of stress on a daily basis."

Stevie studied the dramatic stone and redwood home surrounded by tall trees. "You learn to live with it. Some of us actually fall apart without stress."

"You must if you're willing to do this on your vacation."

"I have weeks of comp time coming. It's no big deal." No big deal. Good. That should keep him in his place. Stevie smiled at the dog jumping around the car, waving his tail frantically. He was an Irish setter, the color of rusty water.

"Ranger seems okay. Maybe Bebe skipped a day."

"Don't count on it. She hasn't skipped one in over a month, including sending love notes to my hotel when I'm on the road." Dusty opened his car door and Ranger immediately moved his head into the opening. "I'm just glad she hasn't hurt my dog. Mike gave him to me when I pitched my first no-hitter."

Stevie watched Dusty rub the dog's thick fur. Strong hands, gentle hands. Hands that could . . . "Mike was as nuts about dogs as you are. His black Lab still sleeps on one of his shoes."

"We ought to talk about Mike," Dusty said quietly. "When he was killed, I was in L.A."

"A deranged parolee got him." Stevie swallowed as her throat tightened. The grief was a year old, yet still fresh. "Just opened fire in front of headquarters. Mike was in the wrong place, wrong time."

"Mike was too young," Dusty whispered.

"Is anyone ever old enough to die like that?" Stevie determinedly pushed down the urge to cry on Dusty's strong shoulder and opened the car door. "We're stalling. Let's go see if Bebe still loves you."

Dusty shoved the dog away. "Damn, you're tough."

"That's what you're paying for. My tough hide and my instincts."

"Instincts?" He ran a finger across her cheek and Stevie shivered. "What do your instincts tell you now, Stephanie Jane?"

Run. Instead she slid out of the car. "My instincts

say to check the premises." Ranger lunged at her in doggy ecstasy.

"Ranger, please," she laughed. "How can Bebe say you're mean? I've never met you and you're killing me with kindness."

"Ranger, down!" The dog immediately sat on his haunches, his tongue lolling as he grinned up at Stevie and stuck out his paw. "He may look like a dumb dog, but he's a great judge of character." Dusty walked around the car to pat the dog's head. "If he's mean to Bebe, it's because she's not nice."

"Well, Ranger, old pal," Stevie said, shaking his proffered paw before she turned to stare at the back of the house, "I sure wish you could talk. You could tell us all about Bebe." Ranger woofed in apparent agreement and followed her up the flagstone walk to the back door. Stevie studied the blinking lights on the pad for the security system. "Everything seems to be working. What's your code?"

"Two thirty-six, B A. My highest batting average."

"Excellent," Stevie said with a grin, "for a pitcher."

Dusty watched her punch in the numbers, then use the key he handed her to open the deadbolt. Her nails were ragged, chewed off. He remembered the teen-aged Stevie's long, perfectly manicured red nails. Obviously the stresses of her job got to her more than she'd admit.

"Stay here. I'm going to look around." She slipped her handgun from her shoulder bag and eased open the back door.

"Damnation!" Dusty stepped back. "Is that necessary?"

"Until we catch your admirer, it is. Stay put," she ordered, disappearing into the house.

Dusty stood next to Ranger on the patio. "I tell you,

boy, Stevie has grown up since the old days. Look at her," he said, gesturing toward the house, "packing a gun and telling me to stay put." Dusty hated to admit it, but it bothered him having a woman protect him, especially from another woman. He'd listened to their horror story about the beautiful TV personality, but his situation was totally different.

Stevie was right. Only an Amazon could take him down. *Or a woman with a weapon.* Stevie's gun was just one of hers. That sassy mouth, curvy body and dark eyes were potentially lethal. He couldn't believe it had been fifteen years since their night together. A lifetime ago. If Stevie decided to crawl into his bed now . . Dusty rubbed Ranger's ears.

"One good thing about this 'obsessed fan' business," Dusty said, grinning down at the dog, "we've got Stevie staying with us. Do you think she'll insist on separate bedrooms?"

"Yes, she will."

Dusty looked up to see Stevie giving him that look again, the look that said she was an inch away from smacking him after all. "You're no fun. Is the house okay?"

"Not exactly. Come here." Stevie turned on her heel. "I wish you'd quit making light of a potentially dangerous situation. Personally, it gives me the creeps to think someone is coming in here seemingly at will." She walked through the kitchen and Dusty followed her into his study. "Look at this."

"My fax machine?" Dusty reached down to pluck a piece of paper from the tray.

"Read it." Stevie looked down at the paper and frowned. "Bebe has your fax number."

" 'Darling Dusty. Pitch a no-hitter for me, baby. One more should cinch you for the Hall of Fame. Don't disappoint me.' " He looked at Stevie. "This woman knows her baseball."

"Not surprising. She's hooked on you, not some rock star. That third sentence sounded like a threat to me. What's she going to do if you 'disappoint' her? Read on."

Dusty scowled down at the paper. " 'I'll be there to see you tonight, right behind first base. Wave to me, lover. I can't wait. Bebe.' " He threw down the note. "Lover? No way."

Stevie rescued the paper and scanned it again. She tossed her hair back in an unconscious gesture that made him want to feel that hair drifting over his body again.

"This gives us two good leads. She or he is getting careless." Stevie snatched up the receiver on the desk phone and punched in a number. "Sally, I'll need some back-up tonight. You can clear it with Mac. Tell him I requested it." She listened for a moment. "Plainclothes. I'll meet them at the first-base side of the Astrodome about . . . ?" She looked at Dusty.

"I've got to be there by five. Game starts at seven-thirty."

"About five-thirty." She listened again. "Great. Tell Rob and Linda to dress for a baseball game." She hung up, then picked up the fax.

"Look, Dusty. The sending telephone number and time are printed at the top. She sent this about an hour ago." Stevie picked up the phone again. "I need a location on a telephone number." She read the number, then covered the receiver with her hand. "They're really quick. Computers make things so easy." She picked up a notepad and pencil from the desk and jotted down some information. "Connect me with Mark Rodriguez." She ripped off the top page and tossed the pad to Dusty.

"Dusty, make a list of anyone who has your fax number."

"Yes, ma'am." He sat down at the desk. Stevie requested a unit to go to the location where the fax originated, once again invoking Mac's name. When she hung up, she came to look over his shoulder, her subtle and definitely sexy perfume surrounding him.

"That's not much of a list," she complained.

Dusty realized he was seeing the professional Stevie, Stevie the cop. She leaned across him to grab another pen and her black jacket hung open. A white top with a scoop neck dipped below the shadow between her full breasts. He wanted to lean forward, to run his tongue down that valley and—

Slow down! You think after fifteen years you can just jump the lady? Last time you saw her, you kicked her out of your bed and broke her heart. He looked at her, so strong, so sexy. If she took a notion to crawl into his bed now he sure wouldn't kick her out.

"My fax number's printed on my business cards. Do you have any idea how many of those I give out?"

"Not many, if you don't want to be called by all your admiring fans."

"But if I'm talking business, we'll exchange cards."

"Exchange? That means you'd have a card from that other person. Where are all those cards?"

"Are you kidding? We're talking about television executives, stockbrokers." He stood and looked through a small drawer in the desk that held the fax.

"Give. Those are all possible leads." She held out her hand. "We're lucky Mac's a friend of yours. This is going to take some man hours." Stevie flipped through the stack of cards.

"You're going to embarrass the hell out of me if you call an executive producer at ABC and ask him if he's been leaving me love notes." Dusty waved his pen under her nose.

Stevie grinned. "Trust us to have a little discretion."

"Hah! I listened to your brother Mike's stories about his investigations. He was about as discreet as a locomotive." Dusty threw down his pen and walked to the window. He stared out at the deck and pool, partially shaded by tall pines.

"Mike always exaggerated for your benefit, to impress you."

Dusty turned around and gaped at Stevie. "Impress me? I thought he was the bravest man I ever knew." He ran his hand through his hair. "There's something wrong with the world if a man who risks his life to put away bad guys is impressed by a jock who coasts through life on a God-given talent."

"Don't talk like that." Stevie walked over to stand beside him. "Mike *was* brave. I'd like to be half the cop he was," she said softly.

"Well, he thought the world of you." Dusty threw an arm across her shoulders. "Mike also told me a lot of Stevie stories. I'd love to see you on the back of a motorcycle."

"Biker babe." She grimaced. "Not one of my favorite roles but it helped me get my promotion." Stevie shrugged off his arm and walked to the door. "Now, I've got to go collect some things since I'll be living here for a while. I'd like you to stay here until I get back. Call 911 if anyone bothers you."

"Wait a minute. How are you getting there?"

"Not very observant, are you, Derrick? We were followed all the way here, though with the way you drive, I'm sure it wasn't easy. Mac arranged it so I could get situated. I'll be back long before we need to go to the ballpark."

"Go ahead. I'm going to take a swim and soak in the spa. Maybe that'll loosen me up." He rubbed at his shoulder again.

"Good. Do you have an extra remote for the gate?" Stevie stopped in the doorway. He looked tired, and faint lines creased his forehead.

"It's by the back door. Unless Bebe took it."

"I'll check." Stevie hurried to the utility room and found the extra remote on a shelf above the dryer.

"That's a relief."

Stevie jumped when his knees bumped hers from behind. She turned, shoving him back with a firm hand on his stomach. She'd let her guard down already, acting more like a friend than a hired professional. It was time to get this back on track.

"Besides that fax list, make one of the people who have regular access to your house. I assume you have a maid service." She waved her hand toward the neatly folded stacks of towels on the shelf above the washer and dryer.

"Maid, not a service. Ivy's not a suspect. She's cleaned for my mom for years." Dusty leaned against the washer.

"The house is beautiful. Spotless, too." Stevie put her hand on the back doorknob. "Write down her schedule. That can help us. I think we can safely assume that, if she had a giant crush on you, she wouldn't have to resort to love notes. She could just corner you in the bedroom one day."

"You've got to be kidding!" Dusty's stared at her in mock horror. "Ivy is like a mother to me. She's more interested in trying to fatten me up or bugging me to produce 'grandbabies' for her and my mother to fuss over."

Stevie checked him out from head to toe. "You don't look skinny to me. As for the 'grandbabies,' maybe she should check California. I understand you've been sowing your wild oats out there for years."

"That smart mouth of yours is beginning to bug me, Stephanie Jane." Moving quickly, Dusty pinned Stevie against the dryer. "I may have been having a good time for the last few years, but I'm always careful when I'm not surprised in my sleep. I have no accidental offspring running around, as far as I know."

"Low blow, Derrick. I certainly wasn't trying to get pregnant that night, and I didn't." Stevie pushed ineffectively against his chest, trying to ignore the intimacy of his hips pressing against her. He was so obviously a man with a strong libido. His closeness and her memories were stirring her own urges in that direction. Bad timing. She had a job to do here and Dusty was the last man she'd pick to revive her love life.

"Get back before I have to hurt you."

"Hurt me? Would you really?" He leaned forward, his hands resting on the metal on either side of her. "Try it," he whispered, brushing his lips across her jaw. "I wouldn't mind a little hand to hand."

His lips hovered near her mouth and Stevie was momentarily paralyzed. One kiss? Just to see? Her body begged for it, her nipples peaked, his warmth melted her sanity. No. Kissing him even once was a sure way to fall under his spell again.

She was too vulnerable where Dusty Derrick was concerned. He didn't really want her. He just thought he could flash those dimples and she'd be ready to jump back in the sack with him. She shoved again.

"Relax, Stephanie Jane." He slid his arms around her and pulled her closer. "How about one kiss for old time's sake."

"I don't think so." Stevie thought about jerking her knee upward, but couldn't bring herself to do it. Instead, she remembered a secret Mike had shared with her about Dusty. She reached forward and ran her fingers up his sides. Dusty's reaction was instantaneous.

"Oh, no!" he gasped, laughing uncontrollably. "Not that!" He grabbed his sides and backed away from her.

Stevie waved her fingers in his face and grinned. "Take that, tough guy. I told you I knew self-defense."

"Unfair. Just because I'm ticklish—"

"A woman has to be smart in her choice of weapons. Now I've got to go." She opened the back door.

"Wait." Dusty put his hand on her arm. "Whatever happened to Rodney? I remember sending you a wedding present a few years ago but then Mike said—"

"His name is Ronnie. As far as I know, he's fine. We've been divorced for ten years."

"That must have been a short hitch." Dusty ran his hand up her arm, under the edge of her jacket sleeve, sending tingles through her.

"Short and not a bit sweet." She stepped away from him. Bringing up Ronnie was as effective as a cold shower. Another good-looking jock, who was probably just as self-absorbed, stood right in front of her. One liaison of that type ought to be enough to last a girl a lifetime. A horn honked. "I've got to run. The natives are getting restless."

"I'll put a phone by the pool if you need me." Dusty

followed her down the walk. "The number's on my business card."

"Good. You can also dial for help if Bebe decides to jump in with you." Stevie waved at the waiting car and pressed the button to open the gate. When she heard Dusty chuckle, she turned.

"This isn't a laughing matter, Dusty. Remember Regina Lampert. Stalkers start out loving you, but if they get jealous or decide you've disappointed them, they can turn nasty fast."

"Jeez, Stevie, you trying to scare me again?"

"Damn straight. Get scared and stay alert. I don't want to find your body floating face down in that beautiful pool." She pointed at the shimmering rectangle of the blue water with a spa at one end.

Dusty shivered in mock terror. "Point taken. Now get going and bring your bathing suit when you come back. Guarding my body will require your presence in the pool." He scanned her from head to toe with a lazy smile. "I suppose it's too much to ask you to wear a bikini."

Stevie shook her head at his look of pure mischief, flattered in spite of herself. "You never quit, do you?"

"You'd be disappointed if I did," he said with a smirk before turning to go back into the house.

Stevie waited until he was in with the door closed, then turned to walk through the gate. It was too easy to be distracted by his playful nonsense. He could joke because he'd never been exposed to the vicious side of a fan gone over the edge. He'd listened to Regina Lampert's story, but hadn't been there, hadn't heard her screams or seen the home of the man they'd finally caught. The stalker's apartment had been a creepy shrine to his victim, covered with mutilated photographs of her.

Stevie walked over to the gray sedan waiting at the curb and carefully closed the gate behind her. She had to protect Dusty from the kind of attack Regina had suffered—for his sake, for Mike's memory and for her own peace of mind.

"Okay, Stevie. Tell me about Dusty Derrick," Margie said from behind the wheel when Stevie settled into the front seat.

Stevie shook off the feeling of doom that gripped her and began a description of Dusty's home guaranteed to satisfy Margie's craving for juicy details.

"You should see his waterbed . . ."

Three

"Slow down. The fax came from a copy center?" Stevie tucked the receiver against her shoulder and grabbed a legal pad and pen from Dusty's desk.

"Yeah, a real busy one."

"Did anyone remember the transaction, Officer Hancock?"

"It's Bob. We were lucky. The clerk is a college student, a psych major who likes to people-watch. She gave a real good description." Bob chuckled and spoke to someone with him.

"What's so funny?"

"Your perp is not exactly a looker. As in woof! Woof!"

Woof? Stevie bet Bob had Alpo for dinner himself.

"All right, Bob. Spit it out."

"She's a strange lady," he said.

"A woman! You sure?" Dusty would be glad to hear that.

"At least she dresses like one. Weird, though, she had on a raincoat, headscarf and dark glasses."

Stevie looked out the window to where Dusty sat in the spa, his face and shoulders browning in the summer sun. "We're in the middle of a drought and a heat wave. Sounds like a disguise."

"Yeah. She was blonde and into heavy makeup."

"How'd she act? Nervous?"

"Rude. Sent the fax with her own hands, wouldn't let the clerk touch it," Bob said. "Paid cash, of course."

Stevie tapped the pad with her pen. "Anything else?"

"The lady was tall, five nine or ten, a big woman."

"Any mannerisms or other distinguishing features?" Stevie made a note to run the description through the computer for anyone with a history of stalking celebrities.

"Kept clearing her throat. Probably disguising her voice."

"Probably. Get your clerk to sit down with a staff artist. I want a composite to show our victim." Stevie knew better than to mention Dusty's name. Cops loved gossip and a tidbit about a famous ballplayer would be too good not to pass on over coffee.

"I may have something better. There was a surveillance camera going. With any luck, we can pull out a couple of stills."

"Great! When you get your report written, fax me a copy at this number." Stevie leaned over to look at the telephone connected to the fax machine. "Oh, how stupid!"

"What?"

"I've been having our victim list everyone who had his fax number and all our perp had to do was look on the phone here."

"What's this all about? Someone sending X-rated faxes?"

"Nothing like that. I can't discuss it, just fax me your report and send the pictures to the Chief of Detectives, he'll make sure I get them." Stevie sighed. "Thanks, Bob. You were a big help."

"No problem, Detective. By the way, my partner says he knows you and to say hi." Bob chuckled.

"Who's that?"

"Randy Markham."

"Hah! I'll bet he said hi. Tell that sorry so-and-so he still owes me fifty bucks." Stevie grinned at the memory. In the slaphappy hours between two and five during a late-night stakeout, she and Randy had made one silly bet after another. "Put him on."

"He won't talk. He says you owe him money."

"No way! That last hooker had roots an inch long. Randy only got points for natural blondes." Stevie laughed when she heard Randy yell something in the background. "I've got to go. Give Randy a kiss for me."

She hung up, her laughter dying. Randy Markham. Another victim of the dirty drug trade. No longer a detective, Randy was back on patrol after months in rehab for substance abuse. He'd been undercover as a junkie so long, he'd gotten hooked, big time. She realized she was nibbling on her thumbnail and snatched her hand out of her mouth. Thank God, she'd never been tempted to go that way. She hated drugs, hated how they ruined lives.

In two weeks she'd have her own task force and the power to try some new methods to run the dealers out of business. And she'd be out of the field, which was more of a relief than she'd thought it'd be.

She stared out the window. One problem at a time. For now it was Dusty. Dusty and Bebe. It was much too easy to treat this assignment like a vacation in Dusty's large, luxurious home.

She could see Dusty stretched out in the spa at one end of the pool, his eyes covered by dark glasses, his head on a folded towel. The sun glinted on his golden hair, his tanned chest barely visible above the swirling water.

Her body reacted, hot and cold all at once. She'd been celibate for a long time. Too long, if the sight of Dusty in a bathing suit made her sweat and fantasize. To be fair, he was hunky enough to make any woman stare. Why else had he been paid a fortune to model underwear? But she wasn't any woman, she was his bodyguard. Why did she have to keep reminding herself of that?

Simple. She'd been so crazy about him as a teenager, she'd done the unthinkable. God, when she thought back to that night . . .

Had she really thought a man like Dusty could be interested in her? Sure, she'd been a cheerleader, full of herself and her fantasies. And she'd been unbelievably naive, taking Dusty's friendliness for something more. No wonder he'd been so angry.

At the time she'd been devastated, humiliated, though of course she'd never told a soul what she'd done. It had been a nightmare waiting for proof she wasn't pregnant. And there had been the phone call from Dusty a month later when she told him she wasn't carrying his child. She supposed she should thank him for that, for being willing to take the responsibility. At the time, she'd hung up on him with a rude reassurance that there was nothing to worry about.

In the intervening years she'd managed to avoid him. Not the most mature approach, but the easiest. Dusty had remained one of Mike's best friends, and it hadn't always been easy.

Dusty reached back to pick up a bottle of suntan lotion, his shoulders flexing. The years had done nothing but improve what had always been a great body.

Hmmm. Stevie tried to ignore a tightening in the pit of her stomach. No, maybe a little lower. Okay, there was no crime in admiring the merchandise. As long as she wasn't planning to buy . . . *Get over it,* she told herself. He was a victim here, someone she had to protect.

Time to slip into the role of Stevie the bodyguard. She knew how to deal with men. Take Randy, for example. They'd spent hours confined to a van or on street corners together. Randy was good-looking and single, but other than a little harmless flirtation they'd always stayed focused on the job.

No one would ever describe Dusty as harmless. Her years of playing by the rules vanished in a heartbeat around him. She'd been an old-fashioned girl, planning to save her virginity for the man she married. Then one night. . . .

Ancient history. She could ignore the pull, even if it was still ridiculously strong. She could even don her bikini, strut her stuff in front of him and remain unmoved. She did need to stay close and she might just teach him a lesson. Crazy, but a part of her still ached from his rejection years ago. Was it too immature of her to want to have him panting after her? Hey, immature or not, revenge could be sweet.

A glance in the mirror a few minutes later almost changed her mind. Dusty already had trouble taking her seriously. The woman falling out of the top of her bright yellow bikini looked like an experienced professional, just not a professional cop.

But she liked it. Liked flaunting her God-given assets. Mac would say she had played a hooker for too long, but she didn't care at the moment. No guts, no glory. The suit wasn't really that daring. Okay, the neckline plunged, but the bottom was downright conservative to disguise her too generous upper thighs.

Anyway, Dusty was used to the feminine scenery of California and his Caribbean island. At least this suit had a top. Sliding on dark glasses, Stevie gathered towels and her revolver and stepped out the back door.

Dusty lifted his sunglasses to the top of his head and let out a wolf whistle. "Ah, Stephanie Jane, I knew you were fun."

Stevie set her towels on the tile. "I never denied it. But Mac would have me directing traffic if he caught me like this."

"You're just doing your duty, guarding my body. Come closer. You definitely need to be closer." Dusty grinned and sat up, holding out his hand. "You're in great shape. You work out?"

Stevie smiled. "Thanks. No, I get my exercise on the job and I play a few indoor sports." She laid her hand in his and slipped off her sandals.

"Indoor sports?"

"Oooo! It's warm!"

"I'm trying to keep my shoulder loose." Dusty helped her down the first step. "Tell me about these indoor sports."

"Karate, tai chi, a little kick boxing."

"Nothing less violent?"

Stevie squealed and stumbled when something cold and wet touched the back of her thigh. Dusty jumped up to steady her, his hand warm on her waist.

"Ranger, go away. You almost knocked Stevie into the pool." The dog wagged his tail, an amber plume in the sunshine, and padded over to the grass to plop down.

Dusty helped her into the spa and Stevie wished again that she'd lost those last five pounds. Only an idiot could call them "love handles," but the way Dusty was smiling, he must like his women with a little meat on them. His women? Forget it.

Settled on the ledge across from him, Stevie ignored his feet tangling with hers. She could stay in control here. Eye his body like he was eyeing hers. Wow! No wonder that body had sold millions of briefs. She smiled and slid her sunglasses over her eyes.

"Thanks, I'm not usually so clumsy, but Ranger startled me. His nose is cold." Shoulders back, breasts high, Stevie stretched her arms along the rim of the spa. Dusty seemed to be in a trance, his gaze fixed on her cleavage. Excellent. Her point.

"I'm not crowding you, am I?" She brushed her toes up his calf. "I can always go swim laps."

"No, don't move." Dusty sounded like he was strangling. He cleared his throat. Yes, she was definitely having an effect on him. "Where do you hide your gun in a get-up like that?"

Stevie reached over and patted the stack of towels. "Right beside me. I'm on duty twenty-four hours a day until Bebe is caught. You know that." Stevie kept calm, even when his foot nudged her hip. Hah! Did he think he could get to her? She raised one knee. That did it. She saw him swallow and stare into the swirling water at the narrow cloth between her legs.

"Warm, isn't it?" Ah, the power of a woman. Use it or lose it was her motto. Dusty was merely a man, after all, and so easily manipulated . . . She leaned over to rub her foot, giving him a better view of her cleavage. He slid his shades down to cover his eyes. Too late. She'd recognized his hunger for what it was.

He reached behind him for a brown plastic bottle. "Sunscreen?" He smiled. "I'll do your back."

"Thanks, maybe later." Stevie snatched the bottle and squeezed a dollop of white lotion into her palm. She rubbed her hands together and ran them over her upper arms, then slowly dragged her fingers across the swells of her breasts.

"God, Stevie." He looked almost desperate, but a sudden beeping interrupted the rather charged silence. Dusty glared at his Rolex then pushed a button to silence it. "I can't believe it. Things were just getting interesting and it's time to go to the damned ballpark."

"Things weren't 'getting' anything." Breathing in the clean scent of pine, Stevie leaned back and looked at the trees towering above them. "I could sit like this forever, I think. So peaceful, so quiet. You have a great place here."

"Peaceful?" Dusty snorted and stood up. "I thought so, but Bebe took care of that."

Stevie watched water stream from Dusty's body. Taut, tanned. Heat flashed through her and she was suddenly in no mood for games. He picked up a towel, blotting water from his flat stomach lightly sprinkled with golden hair.

Stretching out his hand, Dusty hauled her out of the spa, his touch electric, making her heart pound and her cheeks flame. When he gently stroked away thc droplets that clung to the curve of her bosom with his towel, she almost melted.

"We'll do this again, without interruptions," he said quietly. "That's a promise."

"I . . ." Stevie swayed toward him, mesmerized by the smile that played over his lips and the gentle pressure of the towel dipping between her breasts. What was she going to say? Her mind was blank, then she saw him staring and glanced down. Her nipples were clearly outlined by her clinging yellow bikini top. If he moved his hand just a little lower . . . then what? She mentally shook herself and was stepping back when Dusty stumbled into her.

"What the hell?"

"I think Ranger wants in on this cozy scene." Stevie reached down to pat the canine head thrust between them. "Thanks, boy. We wouldn't want to be late to the ballpark. Dusty's pitching tonight and I've got a nut to crack."

"A nut to crack? Very funny." Dusty reached down to flip a switch and the bubbling in the spa subsided. "Ranger, old pal, you're an inch away from a kennel. Your timing stinks."

"Don't blame Ranger. I told you this wasn't going anywhere." Stevie picked up her towel, and reminded herself to breathe. *In and out, in and out.* Finally, she felt calm enough to follow Dusty to the back door.

She had to get over this knee-jerk reaction to Dusty's sex appeal. Just because he came on to her, didn't mean she had to respond body and soul, and have her way with him. Ignoring the lust urging her to do just that, Stevie felt the shape of her gun wrapped in the folded towel. She didn't carry a gun for kicks. She was the bodyguard here and she couldn't let Dusty turn this into some kind of affair.

Dusty stopped at the door, turned and grabbed her shoulders. "There's something between us, Stevie. The minute I saw you in Mac's office—"

"What's between us is an assignment. I apologize for flirting just now. Thoroughly unprofessional of me, and it won't happen again." Stevie reached around him for the doorknob. Before she could turn it, Dusty slid his hands down her back to pull her against him.

"Yes, it will. You're not running off 'til you hear me out."

The man didn't play fair. Pressing his body against hers totally ruined her ability to think straight.

"We have to go." Stevie turned to push him away. Hard to do when her fingers were curled around his biceps, she had to admit.

"Not yet." He trailed his lips across her cheek.

"Stop." Stevie wouldn't look at him, wouldn't kiss him. He finally leaned back.

"This blows me away, Stevie. Hell, fifteen years and there's all this chemistry."

"And that's all it is."

Stevie held herself stiff. She couldn't let him see how his hot breath and gentle hands affected her.

"You wanted me once, Stevie," he whispered. "I can make you want me again." He breathed the words near her ear, sending a ripple of sensual longing through her.

"Dusty, please. This is too fast, too soon." No, that sounded too much like begging. "Stop this. I've got a job to do, let me do it. This is no time for a flirtation. I have to protect you."

She punctuated that with a nice shove into his midsection. He released her immediately, though not without a grumble. Pushing past him into the air-conditioned chill of the house, she had almost made her escape when he grabbed her hand.

"You can do your job and still enjoy yourself."

"Perks?" For a moment, she imagined herself smack dab in the middle of his king-size bed. She took a deep breath and told her imagination to take a hike.

"In Cocoa Beach you rejected me. Fine. Now it's my turn. I'm not interested in combining business with pleasure here. Let's just get dressed and go to the ballpark." She looked him in the eye, then was sorry. His gaze was intense, focused on her. It was flattering, even seductive. She couldn't bring herself to pull away just yet.

"A lot has happened since you slipped into my bed

at the Twin Coconuts Motel, Stephanie Jane, but even then I wanted you. That hasn't changed." He put her hand on his chest. "Feel what you do to me.

"Three Palms, not Twin Coconuts. If you wanted me so much, how come you threw me out of your room?" Stevie felt the rapid beat of his heart under her hand.

"You were too young then, but now . . ." He put an arm around her and pulled her closer. Her knees bumped his and he glanced down between them. "See what you do to me."

Her eyes had a will of their own. My, oh, my. A Speedo bathing suit really left nothing to the imagination. She couldn't help gloating a little. Dusty Derrick, baseball's most eligible bachelor, wanted her. And not just a little, either. Thank God, her own desire wasn't so . . . obvious.

Stupid, maybe, but she did still want him. Even after so many years, she remembered the thrill, the utter satisfaction Dusty had given her. Probably because no man since had come close.

"Control yourself, Dusty! I will not let you talk me into forgetting my responsibilities." Stevie jerked away from him and stalked to her bedroom. Slamming and locking the door, she leaned against it, waiting for his own door across the hall to close. That was telling him, she thought ruefully. Acting like she was still eighteen—and feeling just as vulnerable.

Stripping off her wet bikini, she tossed it into the shower stall in her bathroom, then stepped in after it. She turned on the water and was standing under the spray when she discovered she'd left her shampoo in her suitcase.

"Damn! Damn! Damn!" She pounded the tile, horrified to realize she was crying. What was wrong with her? Stevie Powell saved tears for the important stuff—her brother's death, her partner's murder, Regina Lampert's cruel fate.

Stevie picked up the soap. It was Dusty's fault. He had her on an emotional roller coaster, suddenly trying to reactivate a relationship that had never really existed. A foolish teenager had imagined he loved her. In reality, he had barely noticed her—at least not until she'd slipped naked into his bed. And it had all been purely physical back then. They hadn't known each other well enough to make an emotional connection.

Her disastrous marriage had taught her one thing: A relationship based on fireworks was bound to fizzle quickly. Chemistry didn't solve personality conflicts, or make a toad into a prince.

Stevie pulled on her robe and began to brush the tangles out of her hair. She needed to get Dusty out of her system. That night so long ago *couldn't* have been as great as she remembered. Why not give in? Satisfy her curiosity. She could guard Dusty very well if she slept by his side instead of across the hall.

Stevie frowned at her reflection. Was she crazy? It had taken her years to move past Cocoa Beach. There was no way she'd risk that kind of heartbreak again. She slammed down her brush and picked up her hairdryer. She had to keep her head and keep control. Especially since Dusty didn't seem to be interested in her arguments against having a fling. . . .

Dusty pulled on clean underwear, the brand he'd made famous, and stretched his arms above his head. Thank God, the shoulder felt good, loose. He stepped into starched khakis and pulled up the zipper. Stevie was right across the hall, fresh from a shower. For a moment he imagined her running a towel down those long legs, across those ripe breasts . . .

Damn, she had a great body. He'd seen most of it in the spa. All of it fifteen years ago. Too bad the memory was so hazy. He'd almost convinced himself he'd dreamed it the next morning. Too many pain pills. But a stain on his sheets and a pale pink bra by his bed had convinced him he'd done the unthinkable—had sex with Mike's little sister.

Even if he couldn't exactly remember the details, he'd never forgotten that night in Florida. Seeing her again had hit him hard. Stevie had grown up into a heart-thumping, crotch-tightening package any man would want. Dusty slipped on his shoes and reached for a shirt.

He'd always been restless, driven to succeed. That drive had left him little energy for his personal life. He'd settled for easy, uncomplicated affairs with women who looked good on his arm. The type who had their plastic surgeons on speed dial.

He combed his hair in front of the bathroom mirror. Suddenly his lifestyle seemed shallow, unsatisfying. He realized that he was ready at last to commit to something more, to the right woman. And being back home with his family and old friends had made the urge to merge even stronger. Stevie would fit in perfectly with the kind of life he wanted after baseball. She'd certainly never bore him and she'd make smart, beautiful babies.

Dusty frowned at a new gray hair. If he had to grow old . . . well, he'd never intended to do it alone. High time he settled down and started a family. He could easily imagine Stephanie Jane sassing him when they were both in their seventies. The thought made him smile as he reached for the phone ringing on his nightstand.

"Derrick."

"I'm waiting, lover."

Dusty gripped the receiver.

"Who is this? Bebe?" He heard a soft click. Stevie picking up the extension. He should have let the answering machine pick up. That had kept him from talking to Bebe before. He started to hang up. No, Mac and Stevie said he had to humor her.

"Did you get my fax?"

"Sure. Thanks for the encouragement." Dusty kept his voice calm. "You seem to know a lot about baseball."

"Sure, lover. Do good tonight, Dusty. I'll be watching." The dial tone hummed in his ear.

"Damn!" He slammed down the receiver, then turned when he heard the bedroom door open. "Did you hear that?" He shoved his hands through his hair. "I just had that number changed again yesterday! How did she get it?"

"I don't know, Dusty. I told Mac to re-check everyone working for the security company. Have you told anyone else—"

"Is this *my* fault?" Dusty looked at the caller ID. "Pay phone. I don't suppose . . ."

"She'd be long gone. Does the voice sound at all familiar? Who did you give this number to?"

"Damn it. Other than a few people on the team and my folks, I've kept my number to myself. And, no, I didn't recognize the voice." He picked up a pillow and slung it across the room. "This really ticks me off. Am I going to have to screen all my calls?" He made himself calm down. He'd just decided he wanted to impress Stevie. Throwing an angry fit wouldn't help.

He looked at her, relieved to see her eyes soft with concern.

"I'm sorry, Dusty. Make a list for me of the people on the team. Maybe Bebe is connected with somebody there." Stevie frowned at the telephone. "Don't worry, we'll get her."

Dusty reached for her, but she stepped back. She's only doing her job, he reminded himself. No, he didn't believe that. She'd loved him once, she could learn to love him again. But this Bebe thing. . . .

"Let's get out of here." Aggravated and suffering from his usual pre-game jitters, Dusty grabbed Stevie's hand and hauled her through the house and toward the back door.

"We've got a description now," Stevie said, snatching her purse from a table in the den. "She's a big blonde, about five-nine, stocky and into heavy makeup. Sound familiar?"

"Except for the makeup, that could be our first baseman." Dusty opened the door. Stevie swished past him, her heavy shoulder bag bumping his chest. "You taking that damned gun to the Astrodome?"

Stevie looked at him, her dark eyes serious. "Yes indeed, Mr. Derrick. And I'm fully prepared to use it. By the way, give me that first baseman's name, he could be a suspect."

Dusty couldn't help it. He laughed, deep guffaws that brought tears to his eyes and lightened his bad mood.

"What's so funny? Everyone's a suspect until we've cleared them." She stopped beside his sports car, looking ready to tackle anyone and anything that dared come at them.

"You haven't kept up with the Astros lately, have you?" He was still grinning.

"No."

"Our first baseman makes almost as much money as I do, has a wife and three kids, and has never so much as snapped my butt with a towel in the locker room."

"Okay, we'll cross him off, but the rest of the team—"

"This is not good for my concentration." He ruffled Ranger's fur, then pushed him into the house before he locked the door and set the alarm. "If that lunatic hurts my dog, I will personally go after her with a baseball bat."

Dusty felt frustration get the best of him.

"Maybe Ranger would be better off in a kennel after all." Stevie looked at him sympathetically.

"No, he can't handle a kennel. I'll just have to warn her off the next time she calls. Bebe supposedly loves me. She'd damned well better listen to me. Let's go." Dusty marched to the car, pushing a button on his key chain that made the alarm chirp.

"Wait! I have to check it out." Stevie opened the door.

"Get real." Dusty stepped back as she popped the hood. "I've been here all afternoon. No one could have tampered with it or the alarm would have gone off." He smiled when Stevie struggled with the hood release. "Besides, if this lady loves me, she knows not to mess with my car. Next to my family and my dog, my heart belongs to my Ferrari."

"Make her mad and she wouldn't hesitate to blow your Ferrari to hell," Stevie said, grunting when the hood finally came free.

"Do you really know what you're looking for?" Curious, Dusty went to stand beside her.

"Car bomb."

"Bomb?" Dusty jumped back a step. "Good God."

Stevie lay on the concrete and squirmed under the car. "Until we get Bebe, I'll check your car every time we get in."

Dusty watched her complete an impressively thorough inspection. Competent, serious Stevie, the detective. Sexy as hell and in control. He liked it. Definitely a change from airheads and self-centered starlets.

"Where did you learn all this? The Police Academy?"

Stevie stood, dusting off faded jeans that hugged her curves better than any designer outfit he'd ever seen. He realized he was gawking and strolled over to open the passenger door for her. He couldn't come on too strong or too quick. No matter how in charge Stevie seemed, a woman liked to be courted. He smiled. An old-fashioned word, but it suited his mood. How would Stevie react to flowers, candy, romantic evenings?

"College. A master's in criminology and some special courses with the DEA." She got in the car and tucked her purse beside her legs.

"You're obviously a dangerous woman to cross. I guess I'd better behave." Dusty slid into the driver's seat. He didn't think he would ever get used to the notion that this woman was here to protect him. Despite her hard eyes, she looked too soft, too feminine. But she did carry a gun.

Stevie stared at him, obviously not amused. "I'm trying to do my job here, Dusty, even if I *am* just a woman."

"Aw, don't harp on the gender thing, Stevie. I'm really not a chauvinist." Dusty started the car and backed down the driveway. "I even have a female orthopedic surgeon."

"You let a woman operate on the golden arm? I'm impressed!" Stevie leaned back.

Dusty pushed a button and waited for the gate to slide open.

"Catch Bebe tonight, Stevie. I don't want to waste any more of your time." He reached across to cup her chin, noticing his reflection in her dark eyes. Damn, but he'd give big bucks to know what she was thinking. Was her resistance all duty? Or was she actually over him? She looked away and licked her lips. Not entirely unaffected, he thought smugly.

"We could be good together if you give it a chance." He touched his lips to hers, then looked over his shoulder to back the car through the gate. For once she had no snappy comeback, or immediate denial. He was definitely making progress.

Four

"Dusty! Is it true you've been talking to the Rangers?"

"When you goin' to call it quits?"

"How's the shoulder tonight?"

The moment Dusty had helped her out of the car, reporters had surrounded them. Stevie stepped behind him, scanning the crowd as they moved toward the entrance of the Astrodome.

Dusty rotated his arm for the benefit of the television camera. "Loose and ready to fire." He grinned, then pulled Stevie into the tunnel leading to the players' dressing rooms.

Stevie hurried to keep up with him, grateful when the newsmen amicably stepped aside.

"Wait! Who's the babe with you, Dusty?"

Dusty stopped, jerking Stevie to an abrupt halt. He looped his arm around her waist to steady her, then turned to the persistent reporter with a wide smile.

"Meet Ms. Stephanie Jane Powell."

"Is the playboy pitcher finally going to settle down?" The man thrust a microphone at Dusty.

Stevie stiffened and started to answer, but Dusty's arm tightened. She looked up. Though his smile never wavered, there was a clear warning in his intent gaze.

"Yep, I'll give you the scoop. I'm getting married."

"This *is* a scoop!" The reporter excitedly gestured for the cameraman to shift the camera toward Stevie. "Tell us about the woman who's finally bringing Dusty Derrick down."

Stevie opened her mouth but Dusty snatched the microphone. "Stevie and I grew up together." Dusty grabbed her fist when it started toward his midsection, his smile never wavering. "Moving back to my hometown this year has really been lucky. You know I'm close to breaking Nolan Ryan's strikeout record."

Stevie seethed, reluctantly deciding that a heated denial would do more harm than good.

When the bright television lights finally dimmed, Dusty pushed her ahead of him and through double doors to the area restricted to players and other authorized personnel. She frowned when she noticed two guards barely glance at them. So much for adequate security.

Dusty pulled open a door marked "Physical Therapy" and pushed Stevie inside. Fortunately, the room was empty. Stevie whirled around and got in his face.

"I see I'm not the only accomplished liar around here. What were you thinking? After all my warnings, you announced wedding plans to the media?" Stevie grabbed his arm. "Bebe's going to go crazy when she hears this."

Dusty pulled away and began to pace the room, his hand raking through his hair in a gesture she was beginning to recognize. "You can't know that. I thought it was a pretty good idea. If Bebe knows I'm no longer available, maybe she'll give up." He stopped in front of her and put his hands on her shoulders. "Especially when she gets a look at the competition."

"Get real, Dusty." Stevie swept his hands off her.

They were too warm, too heavy, too hard to ignore. And she needed to concentrate. This was a potential disaster, and now it was time for damage control. What could she do?

"I don't know *what* she'll do, but it's too much to hope that she'll simply slink away in disappointment. Besides"—Stevie stepped closer and poked his chest—"you could have warned me. There would be real headlines if your 'fiancée' slugged you right in front of the camera."

"Calm down." Dusty grabbed her hand. "Call it temporary insanity. I sure as hell couldn't introduce you as my bodyguard." He put his other arm around her and smiled. "Hey, what guy wouldn't want to be engaged to you?"

Stevie felt that pull again. Damn him for looking so appealing. Dimples flashing, a bad boy caught with his hand in the cookie jar. Oh, no, not this cookie.

He was manipulating her and looking altogether too proud of himself. Stevie realized she was swaying toward him and pushed both hands against his chest in self-defense. He just grinned and pulled her even closer, warm and solid. He was making it hard to remember why she was supposed to be mad at him.

"You should have kept walking, ignored the question."

"I couldn't. There we were on camera, you looking so good, so sexy. Hey, I'm just a guy." He ran his hands down her back. "You're my new main squeeze. Get used to it."

Stevie jerked away from him. "No! What you did tonight may very well cause Bebe to go over the edge."

Dusty shook his head but didn't look very sorry. "I told you from the beginning I've got an image to protect. I'm an athlete in prime physical condition except for this bum shoulder. My teammates would laugh at the idea of a pretty woman guarding me." He reached for her again and Stevie stepped back.

"If Bebe tries to hurt you because of this, then what? And stop manhandling me. Next time I'll send you headfirst into that oversized bathtub." Stevie pointed to the nearby Jacuzzi.

"The most violent thing she's done so far is shred a picture." Dusty turned and leaned against the door. "Don't you think you're over-reacting?"

Stevie gritted her teeth. She couldn't tell Dusty that Bebe would most likely be mad at *her*, the other woman. "Okay, maybe you're right and Bebe will back off."

"And if she does?" he asked, tracing her determined jaw with one finger. "You're not just going to walk out of my life this time, Stephanie Jane. We've got unfinished business."

"From fifteen years ago?" She stepped out of reach, every nerve in her body screaming Dusty's name. "You've lost your mind. Quit trying to turn this into a date, Dusty. I'm here to do a job. If pretending to be your fiancée is necessary, I'll do it. I sure don't want to damage the macho image you've worked so hard to create over the years." He was frowning. Good, maybe he was finally getting the message. She pushed him away from the door.

"This is just another undercover operation, Dusty. I'll act like your loving girlfriend in public if I have to, but in private you need to cut out all this harassment."

"Harassment? You going to file a complaint? Sue me?"

Stevie knew she could and should. "No, I realize our history makes you think—" He put his hand over hers when she started to pull open the door.

"Our history. I haven't forgotten it, Stephanie Jane, and I don't think you have either. This is no ordinary assignment for you and you know it. There's still a spark between us. Don't forget that night at the Happy Palms Motor Court when it became a full-fledged bonfire."

Stevie gasped when he pressed her against the door, his body searing her from shoulders to knees. Bonfire? Raging inferno.

"Three Palms."

"I want you, Stephanie Jane. Again."

The word feathered across her cheek, sending shivers through every part of her. Oh, Lord. She felt like a teenager all over again, almost drunk on just the smell of him. And his strength . . . she felt so safe, so absolutely right, held against him. Protected. When his lips brushed her cheek, then down her neck, Stevie finally managed to turn her head away.

"Dusty, stop. Aren't you supposed to be warming up or something?"

"Oh, I'm definitely warming up." He rubbed his thumb across the bump of her nipple through her shirt. "And so are you. Your body is remembering that night, Stephanie Jane. I promise next time for us will be even better. I'll make it last all night."

Stevie trembled.

"This is a job," she whispered. "There are rules."

"You're on my payroll, Stephanie Jane, so I'm making up the rules here. You can guard me and still indulge your desires."

"Now that little reminder was timely." Stevie slapped his hand away and slipped out from under his arm. "Did you think you just ask for sex because I'm your bodyguard?"

"Aw, hell. You know I didn't mean it like that. Mac

insisted I pay you the going rate and it's only right. But that has nothing to do—"

"Shut up, Dusty, before I flatten you. And don't think I can't." Stevie took a steadying breath, her cheeks hot and her gaze fiery. "You just don't get it and I don't have time to talk about this right now." She took another deep breath, aware of Dusty watching her chest rise and fall. He was right. Her body was remembering that night—and craving a replay.

"I've got to get with Cap Hawlsey, head of Astrodome security, about his feeble excuse for security and you've got to get dressed and out on the field."

The doorknob rattled and Dusty stepped back to let the door swing open. A young man stuck his head into the room. "Hey, Dusty. Coach wants you dressed and ready for batting practice in five minutes." He grinned and winked at Stevie. "Congrats. I hear there's a wedding in the works."

So much for keeping that tidbit out of the news. Stevie could have screamed in frustration, especially since Dusty seemed to take the comment as a signal to stake his claim by wrapping his arms around her again.

"Right, Nixon. Go peddle your papers. The lady and I were celebrating."

"Can't do it, Dusty. Batting practice. Coach says you *used* to be pretty handy with a bat."

"Coach can take that bat and shove it—"

"Go on, Dusty, I'll—"

Dusty silenced Stevie with a thorough kiss, one that made her head spin and her knees weaken. His lips finally traveled across her cheek to her ear. "My fiancée needs to sit with my family. Reserved seats, field boxes behind first base. Local TV will probably make a point of scanning the area after our announcement.

Try to look thrilled." Dusty gently tugged on her earlobe with his lips.

The man by the door cleared his throat.

"Come on, Dusty. Coach'll give me hell if I don't come back with you pretty quick."

"Go on, honey," Stevie said, planting a kiss on the warm column of his throat. Part of the act. The loving fiancée. Would Nixon be shocked if she ripped off Dusty's clothes and took him right there on the concrete? *More acting? Sure, right.*

Dusty smiled and winked. "That's my girl. I'll see you down here after the game."

"Be sure to wave at me, honey," Stevie ordered, turning her head when Dusty seemed inclined to kiss her again. Dusty would wave and Bebe would think he was waving to *her*. Bebe. About time she remembered why she was here. She glanced at her watch and hurried to the elevator.

She'd told Dusty this was just another undercover operation. What a crock. He was right. Their history was impossible to ignore. Just the thought of anyone hurting him tied her insides into knots. She had to keep him safe, even if he wasn't exactly cooperating.

"This is impossible!" Stevie shook her head as more and more fans streamed past her on their way to their seats.

"I told you. When Dusty's pitching, we usually have a sellout, over fifty thousand fans." Cap Hawlsey stepped aside to let a woman with a baby rush past him.

"At least five thousand of them are right down here behind first base," Stevie muttered.

"That's right. Since Mac called me, I've put two

more uniforms on the field here." Cap nodded toward the dugout where two policemen stood like bookends. "They're to make sure nobody jumps over the railing."

"Good idea. Would you believe Dusty announced our engagement to the media? He thinks it might make his stalker give up."

"You've got to watch it with these crazies. She could give up or she could go haywire." Cap hitched his pants up over his round belly and looked around. "I wish we could use metal detectors, but the commissioners think it would be bad PR."

"They'd be the first to blame you if there was a shooting here." Stevie studied the crowd, her stomach churning at the thought of gunfire. So many innocent bystanders, many of them kids. But there was no reason to invent worries. Bebe hadn't been violent so far, just in love.

Stevie chewed on a cuticle. What kind of person let a crush go so far? Her stomach dipped and somersaulted. *The kind of person who crawls into bed with her brother's best friend.* Oh, God. She could have ended up like Bebe, mooning over Dusty, sending him anonymous notes.

Stevie squelched a surge of sympathy for the woman. Bebe was breaking and entering. *Like sneaking uninvited into a motel room?* She had to stop this . . . comparison. Stevie had known Dusty for years before that night in Cocoa Beach.

Maybe Bebe knew Dusty too. Maybe she was someone close to the team or somehow connected, so she'd had a chance to be close enough to fall for his charm. It was definitely something to think about. She'd show him the pictures Rob had brought her after the game.

Stevie glanced around, totally overwhelmed. The

poor quality surveillance photos had shown a rather ordinary woman, late twenties maybe. Tall, heavy-set. Unless Bebe persisted in dressing for a thunderstorm, she'd probably blend right into the crowd here.

"I appreciate your help, Cap."

"We do what we can." Cap nodded to one of his men who walked down the aisle toward the lower field boxes to station himself with his back against the railing.

Stevie could see Dusty warming up behind him. With batting practice over, Dusty was limbering up his pitching arm, throwing to a catcher squatting in the dirt.

Several young fans leaned against the rail shouting at him for autographs. Dusty pitched one more ball, then strolled over to sign programs, caps and gloves. The security guard moved closer, but didn't send the kids on their way.

"I guess I'd better get down there. Though Dusty insists I act like his latest girlfriend." Stevie frowned when she noticed a group of giggling girls join the crowd at the railing.

The teenagers were bubbling with energy, showing off perfect figures in skimpy shorts, crop tops and platform shoes. About her age when . . . Stevie flinched. Her jeans were snug enough to remind her to avoid the concession stand tonight.

Obviously Dusty remembered and imagined he still wanted the teenager she used to be. At thirty-something, she felt ancient and in desperate need of a jumbo multivitamin. The girls squealed and giggled, the sound lacerating her already raw nerves.

"The man has no shortage of women," Cap grumbled. "Bebe could be right there, you know." The girls cooed in unison when Dusty began signing the back of their shirts with a marker.

"I doubt it. She's a woman, older, heavier. Those aren't women, those are—"

"Stephanie! What a surprise!"

Stevie turned, her overworked stomach now into deep knee bends. "Mr. and Mrs. Derrick . . . hi!" she said, forcing a smile. Then she saw who walked up behind the attractive couple.

"Mom! Dad!" Hugs all around. Old home week. Terrific. Could things get any worse?

"Gee, Mom, I didn't know you and Dad came to Astros games."

"Of course, honey. We wouldn't miss seeing Dusty pitch for anything." Stevie's mother gestured toward the field. "Lucky for us, Lucille and Doug invited us to share their box."

"You can join us, Stephanie. Dusty always leaves tickets for us at the gate. We've got an extra," Dusty's father said.

"Thank you, I'd like that." Stevie noticed her father frowning at Cap Hawlsey, who quickly walked away.

"Don't I know . . ."

"No, Dad, I don't think so." Stevie grabbed her parent's arm and pulled him down the steps toward their seats right behind the bullpen where Dusty had resumed his warm-up. Cap and her grandfather, a retired police officer, were friends. Her father probably *had* met Cap.

"What are you doing here, Stephanie?" her father asked, glancing back over his shoulder. "Are you on duty?"

Stevie's mother clutched her arm. "Oh, no! You're not, are you, honey?"

"No, I came to see the game." Stevie patted her

mother's hand. Both her parents worried about her job, especially since Mike's death. They'd been ecstatic when they'd heard she'd been promoted out of undercover work.

"Thank goodness." Her mother sighed, settling into her seat.

"You're here by yourself? Sure you're not on assignment?" Her father looked back down the aisle. "That man—"

Stevie braced herself for some serious lying. Her father hated police work, even though his father had risen to deputy police chief before he'd retired. A gentle man who was happiest tending the flowers at his successful nursery, Dad's heart had broken when his only son had been killed in the line of duty.

"I got a ticket from Dusty. I ran into him in Mac's office. We were catching up on old times." Stevie busied herself opening her program.

"Did you hear that, Lucille?" Sally Powell leaned across Stevie. "Dusty invited Stephanie to see him pitch."

Stevie sank further down into her seat and saw Dusty glance their way. She prayed he would have the good sense to keep his mouth shut about their "engagement." Maybe the media wouldn't think it newsworthy and the parents would never have to know. *And maybe it would snow in July right here inside the Astrodome.*

He tossed the ball to the catcher and strode to the railing.

"Hi, you guys! Thanks for coming out." Grinning, he leaned up to clasp first his father's hand, then Adam Powell's.

"We wouldn't think of missing it," Dusty's mother gushed. "And look who's here."

Stevie smiled, her eyes begging Dusty for discretion.

He winked at her, a habit that was becoming extremely irritating.

"It's great to have my own personal cheering section. I'll try to make you proud." Dusty pulled off his dark blue cap.

"Do your best, honey. I'll be counting your strikeouts." His mother patted a notebook in her lap.

"Thanks, Mom." Dusty looked back over his shoulder when someone called his name. "I've got to go."

"Wait a minute, son. How's the shoulder?" Doug Derrick studied his son anxiously.

"Loose and ready to rip. But I couldn't hit jack during batting practice."

"Hey, they didn't acquire you for your bat."

Stevie tuned out a father and son exchange of batting tips and studied the crowd filling the stands behind her. She spotted Linda in an usher's uniform, showing a blonde woman to her seat. Did she look like Bebe? Stevie caught Linda's eye but the operative shook her head.

Rob went by hawking peanuts, his eyes constantly scanning the crowd as he tossed bags of peanuts to excited fans.

"It's almost time to start," Sally Powell announced. "Adam, I need some popcorn and a Coke."

Stevie smiled. Her mother loved baseball, but it was a long-standing family joke that she spent half the game at the concession stand. Her mother was reaching for her purse when a cheer punctuated by loud whistles erupted from the stands.

"What's going on?" Stevie asked. Four pairs of eyes swiveled in her direction.

"Look at the scoreboard," her mother hissed.

Stevie looked up at the huge rectangle that had been showing commercials, cartoons and current baseball scores. The first thing she noticed was that the lighting engineer in charge of the board had let his fondness for pink roses run riot. Then she read the announcement in the middle of the screen.

"Why didn't you tell us you and Dusty were engaged?" Stevie's mother's voice rose several octaves before Stevie was enveloped in a warm embrace. "This is a dream come true."

Stevie was released and Lucille and Sally fell into each other's arms, wiping at happy tears. Wishing she could evaporate, Stevie refused to meet her father's interested gaze.

"When's the wedding?"

Five

"This is a nightmare!" Stevie whispered to Dusty as they pushed their way past the last of the reporters.

"Just smile. We've almost made it. Look, here's the car." Dusty pulled Stevie to the curb where the Ferrari had just rolled to a stop.

"Thanks, Rob. Everything okay?" Stevie asked when the undercover cop climbed from the driver's seat.

"Everything looks fine. Better than fine. That's some powerful engine!"

"Thanks. I'm Dusty Derrick." The men shook hands.

"Great game, Mr. Derrick. I bet next outing you set a new record." Rob winked at Stevie. "Oh, and congratulations on your engagement."

"Part of my cover, you idiot!"

"Stephanie Jane, you keep trampling on my tender regard for you. Ignore her, Rob. This is the real deal." Dusty grinned when Stevie stomped around the car and jerked open the passenger door.

"Looks like you've met your match, Stevie." Rob chuckled when Stevie gestured at him. "Invite me to the wedding."

Dusty promised to put him on the guest list and slid

behind the steering wheel, the car rocking with the force of Stevie slamming the door.

"That was positively the longest night of my life." Stevie buckled her seat belt and leaned back against the leather seat.

"Sorry it took me so long, but I had to ice down my shoulder. The parents give you a hard time?" Dusty waved at the guard by the exit and steered out of the parking lot.

"Oh, no." Stevie glared at him. " 'When's the wedding? We can have a big one, can't we?' That was your mother. 'How long have you been dating? Where's your ring?' That was *my* mother. My God, the questions were endless."

"Tough, huh?" Dusty had to admire Stevie's pout. The sudden urge to lean over and kiss those moist pink lips, to check out the taste again, hit him hard.

"Look, working undercover means I have to lie sometimes, but when it's my parents . . ." Stevie sighed.

"I bet they really worry about you since Mike died." Dusty winced when his left elbow bumped the door handle. His shoulder should have been iced longer but he'd rushed the trainer through his routine to get out to Stevie and the folks.

"Mom and Dad took his death so hard . . . we all did."

Dusty reached over and patted her knee. "I know. I'm even feeling a little guilty about dragging you into this. I could tell my folks are really into this wedding idea—"

"No kidding. Only fast talking kept me from setting a date." Stevie picked his hand up off her leg and set it on the steering wheel. "You owe me for this. Big."

"Whatever you want, whenever you want it,

Stephanie Jane." Illuminated only by the lights on the dashboard, Stevie's face looked soft and mysterious as she slanted a look at him that made the pain in his shoulder zap straight to his crotch.

"I'll add it to your bill."

There was a soft chirp and Dusty stared down at the center console. The mounted cellular phone chirped again. "Oh, no. This is another unlisted number."

"There's only one way to find out."

Dusty picked up the receiver in mid-chirp. "Derrick."

"How could you do it, Dusty?"

Dusty nodded at Stevie. "Do what?"

"Get involved with that bitch. I saw the scoreboard and I saw her on the news too." The hoarse voice cracked.

"Settle down, Bebe. This is you, isn't it?"

"Yes, it's me, you unfaithful son of a bitch." She sniffled. "I knew you had someone. I went by after you left for the Astrodome to leave you a little gift and I found that woman's clothes in the spare bedroom."

Dusty gripped the receiver. "Invading my privacy isn't going to win points with me, Bebe. Quit sneaking around and let's meet somewhere."

There was a short silence, then a deep sigh. "I . . . I can't. But get rid of the woman."

"I've got to have someone."

"Not that woman. I left her a surprise while I was there."

"Surprise? What?" Dusty shifted the phone to his left ear and pulled the car to the shoulder of the freeway.

"You'll see when you get there. Oh, Dusty, how can you marry someone else?"

"Damn it, I can marry anybody I want to. Stay out

of my house and leave my lady and my dog alone." Dusty looked down. Stevie held onto his arm as if to signal caution. Hadn't she warned him to humor Bebe?

"Come on, Bebe. I get lonely and Stevie's a childhood friend. Could be I'm making a mistake. I told you, meet me. Maybe we'll click." Dusty squeezed Stevie's hand. He sounded crazy himself, trying to reason with a lunatic. He'd like to hang up, but that wouldn't do anything but tick the lady off again.

"I . . . I'm not ready."

"Get ready. In the meantime, stay out of my house, quit messing with my dog—" Dusty heard the dial tone and handed the phone to Stevie. Obviously Bebe hadn't liked his attitude. Too damn bad. She had better get used to the fact that he wasn't willing to play her little games.

"You were pretty rough with her." Stevie replaced the phone in its cradle. "And check with me before you make a date with her. We need to plan these things."

"Hey, all I want is for this to stop." Dusty glanced in the mirror, shifted gears and sped back into traffic.

"What did she say?"

"She's not ready. What the hell does that mean? The notes she leaves offer to do anything I want, but she's not ready?" Dusty glanced at Stevie who had a death grip on the dashboard, then looked at the speedometer. He forced himself to ease off.

"She's a sick woman, Dusty. She's got all these fantasies but she can't face reality. That's why she picked a celebrity, someone out of her reach." Stevie let go of the dashboard with a sigh. "What else did she say?"

Dusty steered off the freeway, then stopped at a light.

He tapped his fingers on the wheel. "She's left some surprises for us. We'll see when we get home."

"I'd better call for a unit to meet us." Stevie reached for the phone

"No!" Dusty trapped her hand. He didn't doubt she could easily break his hold, but she settled for a warning look. "She's not there. She said she's afraid to meet me. I don't think there's any danger. And I really don't feel like a hassle with the police tonight. Let's just wait and see what she's done. We're only five minutes from home."

"Mac will kill me if I don't report every incident."

"Mac's not your boss right now, I am. As far as I'm concerned, the less we report, the better." Dusty released Stevie's hand and shifted as the light turned green.

"That's not what we told Mac we would do."

"Tough. You know it's a damned miracle the press hasn't already got wind of this," Dusty said quietly. "We both want to protect our parents. Let the security company handle this. I pay them a nice chunk of change for their silence. And I have my trusty bodyguard close at hand in case Bebe decides to make my acquaintance."

Dusty tried to sound flip, but he gripped the steering wheel until his fingers ached. Maybe he should turn the car back onto the freeway, keep driving until they were far away, someplace safe where Bebe couldn't find them.

"Dusty, we're using HPD resources, we owe them open communication."

"Let's discuss this again after we see what's there." Dusty stopped in front of the iron gate and pushed the remote control. Ranger danced around in the glow from the headlights when he slowly steered down the driveway. "She must have shoved the dog outside when she went in."

"Poor Ranger. I bet he was frantic, trying to guard his turf." Stevie opened her door as soon as the car rolled to a stop. She slid her handgun from her purse and strode toward the back door.

"Wait for me!" Dusty scrambled out of the car and reached the back door just as Stevie opened it.

"Stay back. You don't know for sure she didn't call from here."

"Wait then. Call for back-up." Dusty grabbed her arm. The reality of this situation was finally hitting him. Did he really want Stevie to take on this deranged fan for him?

"Too late now. Be quiet and let me listen." Dusty stayed on her heels as she cautiously entered the den. Damn, he should have bought a gun, taken lessons. But he hated the things. Had never thought he could shoot anyone. But if Bebe tried to hurt Stevie . . . He grabbed a poker from the fireplace, pleased with the weight of it. He wasn't much of a hitter, but he could make a nice dent in someone's head with this thing.

Stevie made a quick but thorough tour of the house. She was a different woman now, hard-eyed, efficient, as she flung open doors. Her gun never wavered. Dusty stayed well back, admiring the fit of her jeans as he told himself he was a damn fool. He should have let her call for help. What if Bebe had jumped her? He was going to have to put his pride, his image, whatever, aside and let Stevie do her job her way.

"Well, there's my surprise."

Dusty moved into the doorway of her bedroom and felt his scalp prickle. "Is it blood?" He stared down at a pile of clothing spattered with bright red.

"No. Smells like paint." Stevie stopped at the foot

of the bed and shook her head. "Bebe's getting nasty. She damaged everything I brought." She stuck her head in the closet and bathroom before returning the gun to her shoulder bag. Wrinkling her nose, she gingerly took a sweater from the pile.

"She got out the scissors again."

"You were right." Dusty picked up an empty can beside the bed. "It's red primer I had in the garage." He pictured a scissors-wielding madwoman slashing and hacking angrily at anything connected to his "fiancée" and swallowed. He dropped the can and reached for Stevie, wrapping his arms around her.

"I'm sorry this happened, sweetheart. We'll go shopping for a whole new wardrobe tomorrow. My treat." He rubbed her back, surprised when she didn't assert her independence again but actually leaned against him. She patted his back too, as if she were actually comforting *him.* And she probably was. Stevie seemed fearless. What in the hell had she experienced to make her that way?

Stevie closed her eyes and took a deep breath. "Yuck! You smell like a medicine cabinet!"

"So much for a romantic moment." Dusty kissed the top of her head and smiled down at her.

Stevie pulled away, refusing to look at the heap of paint-drenched clothes on the bed. "I'd better check the damage in the bathroom. The floor is covered with my makeup." She stepped through the doorway, then stopped, reading the bright red message crudely printed on the mirror. "I'd say Bebe *is* a bit ticked off by your wedding plans."

Dusty looked over her shoulder and read it too. " 'Die, Bitch.' That's it. The woman is a psycho!"

Stevie forced herself to stride toward the hall. "Talk is cheap, Dusty." But the words bothered her, the hatred in them shimmering in the red of her favorite lipstick. She couldn't let Dusty see her agitation. "I can't wait for you to see the surprise she left you." She crossed the hall and swept through the open door.

"Check it out."

"What is it?" Dusty stopped just inside the bedroom.

"We're into red tonight." Stevie went to the head of the bed and plucked scarlet silk boxer shorts from his pillow. "Bebe must be tired of the briefs in the ads." She picked up a piece of pink paper and extended it to him. "Your love note."

Dusty read the note then tossed it on the bed with an oath. "I'm glad you can joke about it! Damn it! I've had it!"

"Dusty, I'm sorry, but at least you're finally taking this seriously." Stevie wanted to move into his arms again, to be comforted by his solid warmth. No, she was supposed to be the rock here, the pro. "Read the note."

Dusty picked it up again. " 'Dearest Dusty. Slip these on. Let the silk hold your. . . .' Oh, yeah, right." He handed the paper to Stevie. "She's not ready to meet me, but she's propositioning me like a hooker."

"Hookers don't put it in writing." Stevie scanned the letter, her eyes widening. "Most men would pay big bucks for the favors she's promising you." She winced at his muffled curse and watched him stomp from the room. She found him in the study, punching numbers into the telephone.

"This is Derrick. I want a security crew out here immediately. There's been another intrusion, as you idiots call it. Why didn't you respond? From the looks of it, this character had plenty of time to do anything she wanted." He frowned at the receiver.

"No, I didn't give my code to anyone! You have

twenty-four hours to make this house safe or I'm suing you. Understand?" He slammed down the phone and rubbed his left shoulder.

"They'll send out some people." Dusty looked at Stevie and shook his head. "Can you believe Bebe waltzed in here and did her thing and they didn't have a clue?" He glared around the room. "I paid a fortune for this so-called security and look what I get. Zilch."

"It's almost as if Bebe does know your code or has the high-tech equipment it takes to override it. That would cost her a fortune, but I suppose . . ." Dusty paced the carpet. "You absolutely sure you haven't shared your code with anyone?"

"No way. She must have that special equipment." He rubbed his shoulder again. "I need to ice down this shoulder."

Stevie glanced at the clock on the desk. "Security's coming now?"

"Damned right. You heard me. If they can't figure out a way to keep that flake out of here, I'll find a company that can." Stevie followed him as he strode to the kitchen and on to the back door to let in a panting Ranger. Frowning, he crouched down and ran his hands gently over Ranger's fur. Stevie felt tempted to reach out and soothe Dusty, to run her fingers through his golden hair, over those strong shoulders.

"Is he all right?" Stevie stepped back when Dusty stood and went to the freezer to pull out the ice bin. He quickly filled a blue rubber bag with ice cubes and screwed on the lid.

"I don't know. I guess so. I'll probably have him checked out tomorrow." Dusty slung the bag over his shoulder before turning to Stevie. "Damn it! I can smell that paint from here! Let's go to a hotel. The

Holiday Inn takes dogs. I want to get the hell out of here."

"We can't leave yet. I want to see how the security company handles things. And we can't rule out their personnel, even though Mac's had them checked out." Stevie steered him to the oak breakfast table and pulled out a chair. "Sit down." He collapsed with a groan. Here came that urge to take care of him again. She felt shaky with the need to hold him, ease his aches and pains. Dusty would love it—but she'd lose all credibility.

Afraid her tender feelings would give her away, she turned, opened the refrigerator and studied its contents. Okay, she could feed him without seeming soft.

"Looks like Ivy left you a feast. Are you hungry?"

"Starved. How'd you know?"

"I ate a hot dog at the game. But I didn't think you had time to eat."

"They lay out a buffet after the game, but you know I had to deal with my shoulder and get out to the parents." He leaned back in the chair, adjusting his ice pack and patting Ranger on the head. The light highlighted the fine lines of exhaustion around his eyes. So many years since that night, yet he could still make her breath catch and her heart quiver. It just wasn't fair.

Stevie pulled cartons out of the well-stocked refrigerator. "You handled our parents pretty well, I must admit."

"Thanks." Dusty chuckled tiredly. "They wanted to believe me."

Stevie stopped pulling open cabinets in a search for plates and looked at him. "You were awfully convincing."

"I just told them the truth."

"Not exactly."

"Isn't it true we met again after years apart?"

"Yes, but that part about discovering how much we had in common was pure fiction."

"But we do have a lot in common." Dusty held up a finger. "First, we both love baseball."

Fighting a smile, Stevie opened a carton. Baseball. Yes, indeed. She'd spent her entire childhood at some ballpark or other, watching Dusty and Mike play ball and fantasizing about Dusty. She'd become uncomfortable with Dusty's cover story, but dealing with the parents and their enthusiastic wedding talk had stirred up a slew of old dreams of marrying Dusty someday. For a few hours she'd been able to pretend. . . .

"Okay, I'll give you baseball. And if Ivy makes your favorites, we both like Italian food."

"That's two. Three, we're both native Houstonians."

"Now that's a reason to get married." Stevie grinned, pulling milk out of the refrigerator.

"Okay, so that one's a little feeble."

"You were supposed to claim you've loved me secretly all these years." Stevie faced him, her hands full. Did he know how long she'd pined for him?

"That goes without saying. And they could see that you'd grown up into a beautiful woman. How could I resist?" He reached out and touched her arm, his hand warm, callused. Stevie shivered and stepped out of reach, dumping cartons on the counter.

"I guess I should feel flattered. But your impulsive announcement has complicated everything. You saw how mad it made Bebe."

"I can call it off."

"And break our parents' hearts? Too late. Besides,

Bebe's furious with me, but so far she's kept her distance."

"So we can stay engaged and I get to pretend I've been struck out by love?"

He was grinning again, so sure he was irresistible. And he nearly was. Struck out by love, and knocked down. All her old feelings for Dusty kept welling up, threatening to overcome her good sense. She looked away, pulling open drawers until she found silverware.

Good sense reminded her that she and Dusty were wrong for each other. The tabloids had chronicled his relationships with beautiful women born to pose for a camera.

Not Stevie Powell. She was used to the shadows, worked best behind the scenes. Standing there in the glare of TV lights had unnerved her. Even worse, it had been Dusty announcing their "engagement." God, she'd spent her teen years and more dreaming of such a moment.

"You're awfully quiet, Stevie. Not plotting some revenge now, are you?" He grabbed her arm and pulled her between his legs. Stevie glanced down. His khakis strained over his muscular thighs and his zipper. . . . She swallowed and tried to move back. Dusty's hand and knees tightened.

"You're in a pretty vulnerable position, Dusty, to remind me I owe you for that dirty trick tonight."

Dusty looked down, then up, apparently deciding she was harmless for the moment. "I took it for granted that you didn't already have something going when I said we were engaged. I didn't mess up something for you, did I?" He ran his hands up over her hips, his thumbs settling on her waist. Stevie put her hands over his.

"I took on this job, I'll play whatever role necessary." His hands tightened. "In public, Dusty. You want to let me finish fixing your dinner now?"

"Not yet. You're not answering the question. Do you have a boyfriend you need to call and reassure?" His face looked serious, but his thumbs were moving subtly under her hands until she realized he'd worked her T-shirt out of her waistband.

"Your concern is a little late." She firmly pushed away. "Are you forgetting this is all an act? When we're alone I expect you to treat me like an employee. Quit harassing me."

"Not threatening harassment again, are you? I thought we were friends." He reached up to adjust his ice pack. "Come on, Stevie, I've known you since you were a little kid."

"I'm not a kid anymore. I'm on your payroll and I'm *not* your fiancée." She pulled a lid off a carton.

"Hell, Stevie, I'm beginning to think you don't love me anymore."

Stevie stared down at a blur of red. She blinked. Oh, yes, spaghetti and meat sauce. Damn Dusty, anyway. He made it sound as if her teenaged infatuation had been a joke. The most traumatic night of her life no more than a humorous anecdote to him now: The night a virgin had crawled into his bed.

She turned to him with a practiced smile. If nothing else, her police training would get her through this.

"Don't worry, Dusty. You're still my hero."

"Then there's hope for us yet."

His smug expression made Stevie long to sling Ivy's spaghetti sauce at him. What was he really after here? Why didn't she put a stop to the flirting, the touching once and for all with a harsh word, a serious put-down?

She rubbed her eyes, suddenly exhausted and more confused than she wanted to admit.

"Frankly, I'm too tired to argue with you. Sit back and I'll nuke something in the microwave."

"Ah, Stephanie Jane," Dusty said with satisfaction, "you'll make a fine wife."

Stevie let fly and left him to wipe the red sauce from his startled face. She stalked out the back door to wait by the car for the security team.

Six

Stevie impatiently watched two uniformed security guards climb out of a white pick-up truck. Only one of them bothered to look at her carefully. The other stepped up to the back door and rang the bell.

"Excuse me, ma'am. Could I ask your business here?" The young guard who had been eyeing her finally approached. Stevie leaned against the black Ferrari and studied the man in the neatly pressed khaki uniform. About her height, thin, with close-cropped light brown hair, he fidgeted with the night-stick at his belt. So this was what passed for security these days. No wonder Dusty had needed reinforcements.

Thank God, they didn't carry guns. This one looked likely to shoot himself in the foot if he got excited.

"You rent-a-cops had better clean up your act. Mr. Derrick is going to sue your company if you don't stop the intrusions."

"What?" The man's pale blue eyes blinked rapidly.

"Hey, Benny! Get in here! That's Mr. Derrick's lady friend. He says she's okay," the other man called from the doorway.

For a moment, eyes narrowed, Benny stared at her.

Obviously he didn't like her attitude. Maybe she should soften her tone.

"It's just terrible what happened. Dusty's so mad." And even madder since she'd covered him with spaghetti sauce. Childish, but satisfying. And more than a little dangerous. She'd stayed outside, away from any possible retaliation on his part, but now loud barking and angry growls drew her into the house.

"Ranger, settle down." Looking harassed, Dusty held the dog by the collar as he lunged at the guards, his teeth bared. "Stevie, put him in the garage, would you?"

Stevie grabbed Ranger's collar, almost jerked off her feet as he sprang at the two men. "My goodness, you're a great guard dog, Ranger!" Stevie patted him on the head and tugged him toward the back door. Just before she slammed it, she looked at Dusty. He wore a clean shirt and his hair was damp. His eyes glittered and she could almost see the promise to make her pay. She led the dog, docile once she'd shut the back door, to the garage. Her feud with Dusty was going to have to wait.

"Guess you're still upset by your visit from Bebe, Ranger. She must have been pretty rough." She squatted down and looked at the dog carefully. His eyes were bloodshot and one whiff of his fur convinced her the poor dog had been maced. His vet definitely should check him out, but tomorrow was probably soon enough.

"Sorry, boy." She gently pushed him through the side door, then returned to the house, following the sound of male voices to her bedroom.

"We've got to report this to the police, Mr. Derrick. This is breaking and entering, not to mention vandalism." The older man frowned down at the soggy mess on the bed.

"All right, Harvey. But wait till we're out of here and don't use my name. I don't want any publicity." Dusty had his hands shoved into the pockets of his khakis, his jaw set. "I'm damned sick of this. What are you going to do to stop it?"

"We could electrify the fence," Harvey suggested.

"I've told you before, that's out of the question." Dusty looked back at Stevie who stood in the doorway. "Kids come by here all the time to see where I live. I won't have one of them accidentally hurt."

"A fine attitude, Mr. Derrick," Benny said quietly. "Don't worry. We'll put motion detectors around the perimeter. Ones that'll turn on floodlights if anyone gets close to the place. Of course, the dog will turn them on too, which could be a hassle. Maybe you should send him to a kennel for a while."

"No way. Ranger stays, but the lights are a good idea. Take care of it."

"Benny and me work the graveyard shift, but we'll tell the day guys to get it done tomorrow," Harvey said.

"Dusty, maybe Ranger should go to a kennel. He was maced tonight." At his stricken look, Stevie moved closer and put her arms around him.

"Damn it to hell," he said against her hair, "if I ever get my hands on whoever hurt him . . ." Stevie gave him a final pat, then wiggled out of his arms. Role-playing was one thing, but this role felt way too comfortable.

"Sorry, Mr. Derrick. Give us a chance to make it right," Benny said anxiously.

"Yeah." Harvey poked Benny in the ribs. "For starters, Benny and me will sit out front in the truck tonight to make sure nobody bothers you."

"Guard the house, but Stevie, Ranger and I are going to a hotel. It stinks in here." Dusty pointed to the bed. "Get someone in here to clean up this mess before we come back tomorrow."

"What about the lady's clothes?" Benny studied them with apparent distaste.

"Destroy them." Dusty looped his arm around Stevie's neck. "Don't worry, sweetheart. We'll go shopping tomorrow."

Aware of her audience and certainly not because she felt the least bit sorry for him, Stevie laid her head on Dusty's chest.

"Dusty," she sighed, pushing her hand into his thick hair. "Who could be so mean?"

"Don't worry, ma'am. We'll get this stopped," Harvey said.

"When?" She glared at both men while surreptitiously pushing Dusty's hand off her butt. "We've been getting phone calls, too!"

"I'm sorry. We can't figure out how she's getting his unlisted number. What do you think, Benny?" Harvey looked anxiously at his partner.

"If she's getting inside, she's getting the numbers here. I saw a note on Mr. Derrick's desk myself a while ago."

"You mean I gave Bebe my numbers?" Dusty stalked out of the room to his study. He grabbed the legal pad on his desk. "Damn. Benny's right. I wrote them down when I had them changed yesterday. I never thought—"

"Most people wouldn't, Mr. Derrick. Our perp's really smart." Watching Dusty intently, Benny stood just inside the door. "Even knows how to bypass your system."

"Then change the system," Dusty growled.

"We'll do what we can. Sorry about tonight."

Stevie pushed past Benny and flung herself in Dusty's arms. "That Bebe is terrible! Imagine anyone saying they love you, Dusty, and then trashing your house and macing your dog."

Dusty patted her bottom again. "Damn right, even worse than throwing food."

At the look in his eyes, Stevie decided it was time to retreat. She backed toward the door.

"Harvey, this is your last chance. Make this house secure or I'm suing. You'll be out of a job. Got it?" Dusty grabbed Stevie's hand before she could make her escape.

"Yes, sir!"

Dusty tugged Stevie out the door and down the hall, Benny following them. "Come on, cupcake. The Holiday Inn has a bridal suite. We might as well get something good out of this."

Stevie stopped in her tracks. "Excuse me?"

"Let's go, honey bun," Dusty said with an intent look. "The guards need to clean up and secure the place." He tugged at her hand. "And I think you owe me for dinner."

"Owe you?" Stevie held on to his right hand, jabbing at a pressure point that made his eyes water. "I think we'd better discuss this outside," she said with gritted teeth.

"Whatever." Dusty sighed and looked at Benny when she released his hand. "Women. I'll never understand them. Sweet one minute and the next . . ."

"I gave up on them a long time ago."

"Can't live with 'em, can't live without 'em." Dusty

clapped Benny on the shoulder and stepped out on the porch. Stevie was giving him that look again. Like she was counting up his sexist remarks to use in a lawsuit. She was damned pretty when she was peeved—cheeks rosy, eyes sparkling.

"Let us know where you're going to be, Mr. Derrick." Benny followed them out the back door. "In case there's another problem."

"I'll put my phone on call forwarding after we get settled. You can reach me, but I don't want to be disturbed unless you catch this crazy." Dusty held open the door, gesturing for Stevie to precede him. "You didn't want to take anything with you, did you, honey?"

Stevie looked up at him and shook her head. "No, even my makeup was ruined. It's so depressing." She sighed heavily and walked to the Ferrari.

"Let's change cars," Dusty said when a muffled bark sounded from the garage. "Wherever we go, Ranger goes." Dusty opened the car door and pressed the garage door opener.

Ranger came bounding out, heading straight for the back door. Benny backed away and slammed the door in the face of the dog's angry barking. Dusty pulled the car into the garage next to a dark green Ford Expedition. Stevie urged Ranger into the back seat while Dusty snatched a bag of dry dog food from a shelf and tossed it behind the seat.

"I'll be right back. I want one more word with those bozos and I need a few essentials."

Stevie sat back in the rich leather seat and entertained herself imagining the ingenious revenges she could inflict on him. Even his stalker would soon lose interest if she had to put up with Dusty's colossal ego, the macho insistence on ordering her around. By the time he flung a gym bag in beside Ranger, she had built up a good head of steam.

Dusty started the car, then studied her for a moment. "Uh-oh."

"Honeymoon?" Stevie snarled.

"We had an audience, remember?" Dusty ventured a hand toward her knee, but she slapped it away. "Our cover story."

"There's no audience now, honey bun." Stevie smiled sweetly. "And don't ever call me 'cupcake' again. This time I grabbed your right hand. Next time I go for your pitching hand."

"Aw, lighten up, Stevie."

"It's hard to lighten up when I see all my stuff ruined and realize Bebe's outsmarted us again." Stevie leaned back, suddenly exhausted. "My condo's not too far from here. Let's stay there."

"All right, now you're talking." Dusty backed out of the garage and around the security truck. Harvey was scanning the bushes around the back door with a flashlight. "What do you think of all this?" Dusty asked.

"Your security?" Stevie turned to be sure the electronic gate closed behind them. How was Bebe getting inside? Maybe she did own expensive equipment. There was no law that said a stalker had to be poor, just obsessed enough to do outlandish things to be near the one they loved. Bebe was definitely serious about this.

"Those guys are doing about as much as I would expect, but they're not cops and they don't have the resources we have." Stevie leaned against the door and studied Dusty in the glow from the dashboard.

He drove as well as he played baseball, with athletic

grace and firm hands. His muscles flexed when he shifted gears. Stevie remembered their long-ago night at the Three Palms and those hands skimming over her body. Even then he'd known just where to touch, when to slow down and when to speed up. She realized that she was squirming in her seat, and to make matters worse, Dusty glanced over at her and grinned as if he sensed where her wayward thoughts had taken her.

"Are you going to tell me where you live or do I have to read your mind?"

Taking a deep breath, she gave him directions. What would he say if she said "yes" to the pretend honeymoon? She wanted him. He wanted her. They were both adults. *And you're his bodyguard.* But indulging herself in hot and heavy sex wouldn't help guard him. Oh, mercy!

Stevie kept her eyes on the passing scenery, counting traffic lights in an effort to take her mind off the man beside her. When they stopped at one, a moist touch on her neck startled her out of her reverie.

She swiped at it and turned to glare at Dusty.

"Hey, blame Ranger. If I want to nuzzle your neck, I'll need more time than a minute at a light."

Stevie let her imagination play with that for a moment. "Green light, Dusty."

"I'll take that as a good sign, cupcake." He ducked her left hand and laughed. "Make my day. Tell me you have a one bedroom condo."

"Nice place." Dusty dropped his bag on the dark green sofa and surveyed the room filled with unexpected splashes of color and plants.

"Thanks." She dumped her purse on a glass-topped dining table and kicked off her shoes.

"You have a knack for decorating, Stephanie Jane. I like that in a woman." He grinned at the look on her face. It was too easy and way too much fun goading her.

"I have a stressful job. I like to come home to peaceful surroundings." She padded into the kitchen in her bare feet. "I'll make you a sandwich, then I'm going to bed."

Dusty walked over to the pass-through into the kitchen and picked up the phone. "Is this your number on the dial?"

"Yes." Stevie was bent over, scrutinizing the interior of her refrigerator. The way her faded jeans hugged her gently rounded bottom fill his head with fantasies. First he'd peel them slowly down those long, long legs, his lips following them down to her slim feet. . . .

"Is that a ring on your toe?" He shook his head and punched in the numbers to put his phone on call forwarding.

"Like it?" She straightened and waggled red toenails at him. "A gift from a friend."

Dusty moved closer, close enough to smell the light floral scent she wore. He reached out and tucked a dark curl behind one ear. She still had great hair, soft, touchable. It always looked a little tumbled, as if she'd just gotten out of bed.

"Friend? Man or woman?"

"None of your business." She grabbed lunchmeat and cheese from the refrigerator and slammed the door with her hip. "Drop the subject, Dusty, or you'll be wearing another meal tonight."

She pulled bread from an overhead cabinet, the gesture outlining her generous breasts in a pale yellow knit shirt. He wanted to reach out and touch, taste them. Despite his best efforts, his memories from Cocoa Beach were a little vague. The pink bra she'd left behind had been a healthy cup size and he'd spent way too much time looking at it, picturing Stevie in it, out of it. Stymied when he'd tried to figure out how to get it back to her without a hassle, he'd finally tossed it in a clothing donation box.

He'd been ashamed of his part in that night. Being stoned on painkillers had been no excuse to let things go so far. He had never forgotten the vision of the very young Stephanie who'd come to him in the dark, the taste and smell of her. Just remembering made him hard. But he'd missed seeing her face go hazy with desire, seeing her eyes close as he pulled a nipple into his mouth, rolled it with his tongue and—

"Huh?"

"I asked you if you wanted mayonnaise or mustard." Stevie turned and looked up at him. "You look like you're in pain. Want some ice for that shoulder?"

"I'm in pain, all right." He took the knife from her and tossed it into the sink. Pressing her against the counter, he ran his hands up her neck, under heavy hair that felt like silken rain against his wrists. He massaged her scalp, his hands angling her head so she had to look up at him.

"Do you ever think about that night, Stephanie Jane?"

Stevie didn't pretend to misunderstand him. She took a breath and felt her breasts brush his chest. It was tempting to lean a little closer, to ease the ache. Oh, God, had she thought about that night? She'd tried to forget it, had succeeded long enough to think she was in love with Ronnie Harmon.

But Ronnie had never been Dusty. Okay, maybe her

memory had turned Dusty into a fairy-tale lover, someone impossible to compete with. Whatever the reason, her father had lamented that it had taken longer to pay his MasterCard bill for the reception than she'd stayed married.

"Well?"

Stevie relaxed as his strong fingers gently caressed the tight muscles at the back of her neck. "How could a girl forget her first time?"

"Not a girl. You were a woman. You insisted on that, as I recall. Who took you to your senior prom?"

He was so close she could see the stubble on his jaw, feel the warmth of his breath against the hair at her temple.

"A friend of Mike's. I always did go for older men." She thought briefly about shoving him away. He was taking liberties, standing so close, touching her. But his hands were magic, working the tension out of her like he'd work the stitching on a baseball. She rested her hips against the counter, bracing herself with her hands and stretching her neck so he could get the kinks out. She bit back a moan of pleasure.

"Which friend? Mike's friends were my friends." He was frowning. Good.

"Tommy Delhomme."

"Damnation, Stevie. Tom used to brag about the collection of panties in his glove compartment. You didn't—"

"You're so pretty when you're jealous." Stevie grinned when he muttered a pithy comment. "It's absolutely none of your business whether I gave Tommy a souvenir of our evening or not. He was a great dancer, fun. A perfect prom date."

"You left me a souvenir."

"I know, I couldn't believe—" Her breath whooshed

out of her when Dusty pulled her closer, crushing her breasts against him. Stevie looked up, ready to hurt him if he really thought he could force her to do anything. Then she saw his eyes. He wanted her, his eyes shimmering like the ocean in a hot summer sun.

"Stop." The word hissed out of her, sounding uncertain.

"Just a taste." He leaned down and brushed his lips across hers, nibbling, exploring, coaxing, yet stopping short of deepening into a real kiss. A taste. A taste that made her hungry for more, for everything—

"What?" Dusty frowned and raised his head.

"The phone. I'll get it." Stevie pushed him back and grabbed the receiver. "Sure, just a minute." She handed it to Dusty. "Benny from the security company." Thank God for the interruption before she did something incredibly stupid like pulling Dusty down onto the tile floor and letting him—

Stevie turned her back on him, slapping together a sandwich in record time. Her hand shook as she mangled the cheese. This was ridiculous. She had faced off with drug dealers. Handled murderers with more control and fewer nerves. She poured a glass of milk and slid the plate and drink toward him just as Dusty slammed down the receiver.

"What's the matter?"

"Just the usual. No sign of forced entry. The police came and took pictures, scratched their—" He gave her a rueful look. "Sorry, I forget you're one of them."

"Hey, you're frustrated." Stevie handed a salivating Ranger a piece of cheese. "I need to show you the picture we got at the copy center. See if you recognize her." She opened her purse and pulled out a picture. "Here. Know her?"

Dusty stared at the grainy photo. There *was* a resemblance . . . but to whom? Something hung there just out of reach. "Hell, I don't know. Could be anyone in a get-up like that."

"Yeah, Bebe's smart."

"Smart? Or are we being stupid?" He put a hand on her shoulder. "Not you, of course. The security company." He yawned. "Man, I'm bushed. Ready for bed?" Stevie stared at him for one brief, hopeful moment. Was she considering . . . ?

"My study has a sofa bed. I'll set it up while you eat."

"What? No rerun of the No Palms Motor Court?" Dusty grinned as Stevie hastily put the sandwich makings back into thc refrigerator, her face pink. Where was the gutsy undercover cop now? She looked like a flustered woman who didn't know where to look.

"Three Palms," she muttered, "and no, no reruns."

She hurried down the hall while Dusty settled at the breakfast table, setting his plate on a colorful placemat. Ranger stuck his head in his lap and Dusty gave him a pat before ordering him to lie down.

Poor Bebe. Her stalking had done nothing but hclp him find Stevie again. And it couldn't have happened at a better time. He'd dreaded his approaching retirement and fortieth birthday and had tried to re-evaluate his life and set new goals. Stevie had mocked his reasons for the pretend engagement, but a lot of marriages started with less.

They were perfect together. And their parents had talked of grandchildren . . . maybe it was time. He envisioned a family of his own, and imagined coaching his son's Little League team or watching his daughter stumble through her first dance recital. A dark-haired little girl with long legs and bright eyes.

Stevie strolled back into the room, her hair pulled

back in a ponytail. She looked about eighteen again and she was smiling as if she knew a secret. Dusty realized he was smiling too, feeling a kind of peace here with Stevie he'd never felt before.

He wanted to kiss that smiling mouth, explore that voluptuous body, with the lights on and a clear mind this time. She'd loved him once enough to give him her virginity. Had it been too long ago to stir those feelings back to life? Dusty threw back his chair and met her halfway across her living room. He cupped her face in one hand, her skin warm and smooth under his fingers. Her dark eyes were wide, questioning and more than a little wary. He didn't blame her. Perhaps he was moving too fast here, but he couldn't help himself.

"Stephanie Jane Powell, will you marry me?"

Seven

"Knock it off, Dusty. There's no audience to appreciate your performance."

"No, I mean it. Marry me. We'd be good together."

Stevie sank down into a chair. "You're nuts."

"Is it nuts to want to take care of you?" He ran a hand through his hair. "Hell, Stevie, when I think of you facing off with drug dealers and psychos. . . . As my wife you could quit all that, concentrate on making us a home, starting a family. We're not getting any younger, you know."

He was actually smiling. Thought he was doing her a favor. Temporarily speechless, Stevie looked down at her hands. She could wrap them around his throat and—

"You've got it all figured out, don't you?"

He reached for her hand. "Hey, it makes sense. We've got this great chemistry, common background—"

Stevie stood up and stalked into the living room. "Good God, Dusty, we just met again this morning. Are you saying it was love at first sight?" She turned to look back at Dusty. His eyes seemed to see right through her. God help her, she hoped not. For a minute there her heart had leaped around in her chest like Ranger greeting a friend.

"Why not? Zapped by Cupid's arrow. I told you I felt something there in Max's office."

"Maybe you had heartburn." Stevie put her hand out when he grinned and reached for her. "Stay back." She realized she was trembling. "Damn it, Dusty, you can't ask to marry me just like that!"

"Why not?" Dusty was so impossibly handsome it took her a moment to get her thoughts in some kind of order. "I had planned to get married sooner or later."

"So why haven't you done it before?"

"Maybe since that night at the Sweaty Palms Motel, no other woman's measured up."

"You can't even remember the name of the damned place. It's obvious to me you've been hit in the head with a baseball bat at some point in your career." Stevie rubbed her forehead. She would not cry, damn it.

"Now, Stephanie Jane. Give it some thought."

"Right. As if you did. Our chemistry, as you call it, isn't a real good reason to get married." She paced around the sofa, couldn't bring herself to sit. She had to ignore the part of her shrieking with joy, urging her to throw herself at him and consummate the deal before he could change his mind.

"It's a start."

He was watching her with a faintly wicked grin.

"You think this is funny? Yeah, a real laugh riot." Stevie cleared her throat, satisfied that she'd at least managed to wipe the smile off his face. "Trust me, a failed marriage is no joke. Next time I take the plunge, I intend for it to last forever."

"Good. Because I plan to spend the rest of my life with you, Stephanie Jane. Divorce is not an option."

Oh, he looked serious now. And the fact that he wanted a marriage to last forever touched something deep inside her.

"For argument's sake, let's pretend you haven't completely lost your mind. You don't know me, Dusty. Not really." Her knees wobbly again, she dropped onto the couch.

"Sure I do." He sat beside her and grabbed her hand. "You're a beautiful, mature woman with a successful career. Mike kept me posted on your progress up the ranks. It impressed the hell out of me when you made detective."

Stevie stared at him. "Thanks, Dusty. But do you have any idea what it took for me to get that promotion? What I've been doing for the last ten years? I hustle hustlers, have to be meaner and sneakier than anyone on the street. It's not easy and I'm damned good at it." He just didn't get it. He was still smiling, evidently convinced that he was doing her a giant favor by offering to rescue her from her life.

"Get this, Derrick. I'm not looking for a knight on a charger to ride up and rescue me." She took a deep breath. "I'm fine just the way I am." To her horror, her voice cracked and tears suddenly clogged her throat.

"Sure you are, sweetheart. That's why I love you." He put his arm around her, but Stevie held herself stiff. She was an inch away from an all-out crying jag.

"I'm sorry, but I don't believe you." Stevie slid out of his arms and off the couch. She took a shuddering breath and pressed her hands to her eyes for a moment. Finally, she turned to look at him.

"I'm taking Ranger out for a walk. Do us both a favor and be in bed before I get back or I can't promise that I won't do something we'll both regret." Good.

He'd finally stopped smiling. Maybe, just maybe, she'd finally gotten through to him. Love. Marriage. After less than twenty-four hours together? And years apart? No way.

She opened the front door and coaxed Ranger outside. The air was warm, sultry, and it took her a full five minutes of hard walking to calm down. Fortunately Ranger was well trained, staying close and taking care of his business like a gentleman.

Stevie stopped beside the deserted pool in the middle of her apartment complex and stared down into water lit by submerged lights. Turquoise—the color of his eyes. The water blurred and she wiped her tears, speaking softly to no one in particular.

"Damn it, Dusty, you're fifteen years too late."

When she finally returned to the condo, she was relieved to see Dusty had taken her advice and gone to bed. She felt almost numb with exhaustion, yet not numb enough. Crawling into her bed, she stared at the ceiling for a long time, remembering everything. Cocoa Beach. This ridiculously long day.

She couldn't take Dusty's proposal seriously. It had been an impulse he'd soon regret. And whether he was serious or not, she was an adult, not a lovestruck teenager. She could see clearly now. Dusty was all wrong for her. She was wrong for him, even though her heart ached for him, had ached ever since Dusty had rejected her. It was too late for him, for them. Much too late. . . .

She heard gunshots . . . far away. Then Stevie bolted up in the bed, her heart pounding, tears running down her cheeks. The bedroom door creaked open.

"Stevie, you okay?" Dusty sat down and held her close.

She shuddered. Her partner Riley had seemed very much alive in her nightmare. Until the gunshots. She leaned against Dusty, suddenly boneless. He rubbed her back and murmured soothing nonsense into her ear until the dream slowly faded.

Dream. No, a terrible memory of the night Riley had died, the stakeout that went wrong. During the day if she kept busy, she could go almost an hour without thinking about it. But at night . . . The funeral this morning had brought it all back. She shuddered again.

"Want to tell me about it?" Dusty said quietly.

"Trust me, you don't want to hear about it."

"I can take it." He leaned back against the headboard and settled her into the curve of his arm. Her cheek rested on his chest, warm, hard . . . bare.

She glanced down. The briefs he'd made famous covered him, fortunately.

Maybe she should tell him about Riley. He thought she could just walk away and forget her work. And there were times when she'd like nothing better. The responsibility, the danger, the guilt could overwhelm her. But walking away was gutless. She owed it to Riley, her partner on the HPD's task force on drugs, shot dead by a dealer. Her upcoming promotion meant everything to her. If she could at least slow down the stream of drugs hitting Houston streets every day, then maybe Riley would rest a little easier.

"I was dreaming about the guy we buried today. Riley." Dusty smoothed her hair back from her forehead, the gesture soothing, not sensual, and she relaxed against him.

"Riley was a character, always wisecracking. Flirting." Stevie sighed. She realized her hand was resting on his chest and jerked it away.

"We were setting up a dealer. The creep made a play for me. Riley jumped in too soon and he got shot." It sounded so simple that way. No smell of creosote and rotting garbage from the nearby alley, no screaming sirens, no metallic taste of sweat, tears and fear.

"He died saving me. I should have been able to handle it. Should have been ready with my own gun. If I—"

"Hold it." Dusty's arm tightened around her. "I assume this guy—Riley—was your, what do you call it, your backup?"

"Yeah."

"Then you weren't supposed to handle it by yourself. The man was doing his job and knew the risks. Am I right?" He looked down, so close. There were crinkles around his eyes, eyes full of sympathy, caring. Like a friend. *Dusty, your friend?* She liked the idea, much too much.

"But—"

"Am I right or not?"

"Yes, you're right. We both knew the risks. But I should have been able to distract the dealer, at least spoil his aim."

"Sounds like you're second-guessing the situation. Like me rehashing a pitch. You can't rewrite your life. You just have to do your best and live with the consequences."

Stevie looked up, itching to trace the frown line between his brows. "You're sounding downright philosophical, Dusty." She let him draw her closer and relaxed against him. This felt so right, too right and she was dangerously close to falling under his spell again.

She closed her eyes and thought back to the night Riley had been killed. Second-guessing. Yes, she was good at that, and often so tangled up in "if onlys" she could hardly sleep at night.

Riley had been a pain in the butt, a sexist joker who'd loved to rile her. Part of her guilt came from the fact that she'd never really liked him. But he'd been a good cop. Had known the job inside out. And he'd made a fatal mistake by trying to protect her before reinforcements had arrived. Stevie bit her lip to keep from sobbing.

"Hey, you going to sleep on me?" Dusty shook her gently.

"Maybe." Stevie pretended to yawn to make him go away. "Thanks. You helped, really."

"You grateful enough to let me bunk in here?"

Stevie looked up. His eyes were twinkling. He was teasing. If he hadn't been, it would have spoiled everything. Canceled out all that sympathy and good advice. She smiled at him.

"Back to the sofa, sir." She pushed at him and he slid over and stood up. She stared up at over six feet of one hundred percent heart-stopping, willpower-melting male with only five percent of his perfect body covered by white cotton. Her body was humming again.

"A good-night kiss?" He leaned down, one hand on the headboard, and traced the curve of her jaw.

Stevie felt the heat of his finger on her and knew a kiss was risky. But her willpower had gone somewhere south of her bellybutton. Her eyes closed and she felt warm lips meet hers lightly, tenderly, exploring without invading. She shivered and reached up, feeling a small dent in his smooth shoulder. Surgery scar.

He teased her lips open, pushing his fingers into her hair and angling her head until they fit . . . perfectly. Heat flashed through her and Stevie tried to ignore her body's longing for more. Finally, she found the will to push him away.

"Good night, Stevie." Just like that he was gone, leaving her panting, aching, wondering . . . still tasting him.

He had asked to marry her. She forced herself to remember all the reasons why that wasn't a good idea. But every reason seemed feeble compared with the prospect of sleeping beside Dusty every night and having that incredible body whenever she got the urge. And reason took a hike when she imagined making babies with blond hair and blue eyes, spending her days being a mommy and devoted wife. *What's wrong with this picture?* Stevie Powell didn't fit into it.

She'd spent years toughening herself to keep the pain of her job from breaking her heart. She couldn't just shed that toughness at Dusty's whim and walk away. Her promotion might give her the clout to make a real difference. How could she have her own kids when there were so many creeps out there hurting other people's kids? It didn't make sense.

Besides, she loved getting the bad guys out of decent people's way, even when she was absolutely terrified. And when everything worked out right for the good guys . . . there was no adrenaline rush like it.

She rolled over and punched her pillow. Dusty didn't understand her. Didn't know her. He just wanted her. Okay, so that was nice. More than nice. It was downright seductive. *Get over it. You're with him to do a job, remember? If only . . .*

Damn. More "if onlys." Dusty was right, it was too late to save Riley. But it wasn't too late to save Dusty. She'd told him she would handle Bebe and that had to be her focus.

Stevie pressed a hand to her queasy stomach. Dusty had taken a huge risk announcing their engagement. And she really shouldn't have gone along with it. She'd been too sure that she could handle Bebe.

She pressed her face against a pillow, breathing in fabric softener and a whiff of that delicious aftershave Dusty wore. If she lost him like she'd lost Riley . . . her heart jumped into her throat and she felt seriously nauseated. Maybe she should get someone else in here. Someone who could concentrate on protecting Dusty instead of playing games with him.

Games? Touch me, touch me not? Dusty wouldn't allow a male bodyguard, and a woman with any kind of sex drive at all would have the same problem concentrating that she was having. She moaned and rolled over to stare at the ceiling.

She couldn't delegate this, Dusty's safety was too important. *And you can't stand the thought of another woman with him,* said a small voice in her head. She ignored it. Besides, what would the media think? Ah, finally a valid reason. She could do this. She just had to concentrate.

But Dusty wanted her. And when he decided he wanted something, he went after it. She'd have a hell of a fight on her hands to resist that charisma, that light in his eyes, that . . . everything.

She had to resist, even when she was secretly gloating that he'd picked her, ordinary Stephanie Jane Powell, when he'd finally decided to take a wife. He had it all figured out. He would take care of her—own her. Too bad, because she had no intention of belonging to anyone.

No wonder his proposal had sent her into a tailspin. She was a modern woman, independent, self-sufficient, and Dusty was clearly looking for an old-fashioned kind of wife.

Living with her, however briefly, should open his eyes. She'd just have to show him how far she'd come since her days as a teenaged virgin.

Eight

Stevie crawled out of her usual nest of pillows and groped for the phone.

"Hello."

"Stephanie, I'm glad you're home."

"Mom? What time is it?"

"It's after nine. Wake up and talk to me. I'm so excited I hardly slept." Her mother laughed. "Can you come for lunch today? And bring Dusty?"

Stevie groaned. "Do I have to do this before coffee?"

"You bet. I couldn't ask you in front of Lucille, but how on earth did you finally snag Dusty Derrick?"

"Hey, he finally saw the light and realized Mike's little sister had grown up." Stevie sat up and brushed her hair out of her eyes.

"I know you're thrilled. The way you mooned over him when you were a teenager. So embarrassing!"

"Mother!" Stevie groaned and collapsed against the pillows. "You never said a word."

"What could I say? 'Don't drool on the man, darling, you're getting his shoes wet.' At least Dusty didn't have a clue." Her mother laughed again, obviously delighted at the prospect of her daughter getting married again. "I swear I slept with one eye open the whole time we were in Florida that spring."

One eye open? Not quite. There'd been a duet of snores coming from her parents' bed before she'd dared sneak out of their room. And for all her hindsight, her mother hadn't noticed her daughter's guilty look the next day.

"Well, I've got him now."

"You sure about this one?"

"Trust me, this thing with Dusty is nothing like the Ronnie fiasco." Uh-oh, she'd done it now. Stevie closed her eyes, mentally counting to ten. She was only to three when—

"This 'thing' with Dusty? Stephanie Jane, I hope you're talking about a mad, passionate love affair. Don't settle for anything less."

"Hey, I've always loved him. You know that." If only she didn't. Stevie looked up to see Dusty grinning at her from the doorway. Dressed in jeans and nothing else, he looked like a Greek god, holding a cup of coffee out to her. She took it gratefully while her mother raved about her future son-in-law.

"Mom, why don't you just adopt him?"

"Behave, Stephanie. Now I want to hear about your plans. When will you quit your job?" Oh, great. Here came the police-work-is-too-dangerous argument again.

"I'm not. Dusty realizes I'm a modern woman with a career." He sat on her bed and reached forward to arrange her hair over her breasts. She pantomimed tossing her coffee in his face and he quit with a grin. She pulled the sheet up to her neck even though the nightshirt she wore was thick flannel and totally sexless.

"But when you have children . . . you are planning

a family, aren't you? I want to be a grandmother, Stevie. All my friends—"

"I know, Mom. You've told me a thousand times." Stevie sipped her coffee and focused on Dusty's bare chest. Hmmm. Making grandchildren didn't have to be a chore. She dragged her eyes away from Dusty's amazing musculature and focused on her coffee cup.

"Time's passing, Stevie. Old eggs can be a problem."

"What?"

"You heard me."

"Old! I'm only thirty-three." Stevie set her coffee on the nightstand to fend off Dusty's hands trying to pull down her sheet. "Mom, I've got to go. Dusty's here and—"

"You let him see you in the morning before coffee? Don't scare him away before you can get him to the altar, honey."

"Don't worry, I just sleep with a bag over my head. It makes breathing difficult, but—" Dusty snatched the receiver and stood up.

"Good morning, Mrs. Powell. You have a beautiful daughter, even in a Macy's bag." He grinned and stepped away from Stevie's lunge for the phone, still talking to her mother.

"Oh, I am." He dodged Stevie's swipe, stretching the phone cord until he was almost out the door. "As soon as baseball season's over, we'll all sit down with a calendar."

Stevie thought about just unplugging the phone. Why bother? Her mother certainly wasn't going away. This was temporary anyway. She felt a stab of disappointment. Time for a reality check. They *were* acting here. Dusty had said the right thing. There was another month before the season was over. And at the game the Derricks had made it clear their only son's wedding would be the kind of major production that could take a year to put together.

Her own folks had jumped right into planning a wedding extravaganza. Apparently MasterCard had been neglected lately and business was booming at Powell's Green Thumb Nursery. Her first marriage obviously didn't count and the second send-off for Stephanie Jane Powell would be front-page news—at least in the sports section. Even her father had chimed in excitedly during the champagne punch versus open bar debate.

Things were totally out of control. Stevie settled back against the headboard. She would just have to pretend to go along with all the plans until Bebe was caught and she and Dusty could stage a break-up. Oops, there was that disappointment again. How many reality checks did she need? Dusty was listening again.

"Don't worry, Mom, I'll make an honest woman out of her as soon as she'll let me." He hung up the phone, looking altogether too pleased with himself.

"An honest woman? Mom?" Stevie threw a pillow at him. "Weren't you just too cute?"

He caught the pillow and tossed it aside. "Cute? Was I cute?" He sat on the edge of the bed. "Is that a good thing? A manly thing? Puppies and babies are cute." He growled and reached for her. "I think I'd rather be dangerous."

Stevie warded him off with a hand in his grinning face. Manly, oh, yes. His cheeks were rough with a morning beard and his muscular chest had a very attractive sprinkling of hair that arrowed down into the snap of his low-slung jeans. Dangerous. *Very* dangerous.

"In this case, cute is definitely bad. How can you say you'll make an honest woman of me with a straight face?" The man just wouldn't keep his hands off her. Stevie scooted to the far side of the bed, too aware of the fact that, as thick as her faded blue flannel nightshirt was, it was all she wore.

"I do want to marry you. I told you that last night."

"And what I want doesn't matter?"

Dusty trapped her against the headboard, his body angled over hers. "Of course it matters." He grinned down at her, his chest right up against her breasts. Her nipples stood at attention, thrilled with the pressure.

"What do you want, Stevie?" He quit smiling and cupped her chin in his hand.

You, she wanted to say. Her brain battled for control, losing when Dusty shifted his weight to bring her snug against him, one thigh between her legs. Ah, he was so decidedly male. Mother Nature had a certain part of her screaming, "Take me! Take me!" She told her body to shut up and pushed at his chest. That only made things worse. Her fingers loved the smooth heat of his skin, itched to trace a small brown nipple.

"Get off," she finally managed to say breathlessly.

He shook his head sadly and slid off her. "You know I'd never force myself on you, but I remember . . ."

"I don't," she lied. "The entire episode is shrouded in the mists of time. Blanked out. Forgotten."

"I don't believe you." He reached out and palmed her breast, nudging her aching nipple. Stevie gritted her teeth and lifted his hand away.

"Okay, now you know. I'm not an honest woman, Dusty. You can't believe a word I say. An undercover cop lies for a living and I'm an expert."

Dusty rolled off the bed and to his feet. "And your point?"

Stevie wracked her brain, sure she had one. "My point is that you making up a story for the reporters was bad enough. Could we try to keep our parents out of it? Anyway, we need to get our stories straight and stick with them, no embellishments. Sooner or later, we're going to slip up."

"Fine. Just remember Cousin Trish looks sallow in pink."

"What?"

"Mom's sure you'll want her to be your maid of honor. She suggests green or blue." Dusty laughed and dodged two more pillows. "You sleep with a hell of a lot of pillows. Lonely?"

Stevie wished for a big stick, a baseball bat—okay, even the lamp on the nightstand was looking good. "Cute and a comedian. I can't stand it. Get out of my room."

"In a minute." He picked up a pillow and held it in front of him like a shield. "Through with your tantrum?"

"Tantrum? You haven't begun to see a tantrum." Stevie slipped out of bed, tugging the nightshirt down to her knees as she advanced on him. "Out of my bedroom."

"Gee, not a morning person, are you?" He held his ground, even when her right fist landed in the middle of the pillow.

"Why you—" Stevie grabbed her pillow and flung it on the bed. He grinned and backed out of the room.

"Relax. Drink your coffee. Then get dressed. I'm making an appearance at Children's Hospital and then we can do our shopping. I owe you a wardrobe and you definitely need some sexier night wear."

Stevie slammed the door in his face. Not a morning person? Make an honest woman of her? Sexier night wear? The man's sins were piling up. How much was he paying her? Not nearly enough for this kind of aggravation.

But shopping wasn't a bad idea. Dusty had deep pockets and owed her a wardrobe. Stevie picked up her tepid coffee and drained it even though it lacked its usual two packets of artificial sweetener. Dusty would have to pay for tormenting her. Dearly.

"Really, Dusty, let's just forget it. I can go shopping by myself sometime. Just give me your credit card."

"No way, Stephanie Jane. I'm afraid to unleash you without supervision. Until we were interrupted, I could tell this was going to cost me, big time." Dusty smiled, but she knew he was pretty frustrated. The price of success. He only had to step into a store to be immediately surrounded by curious fans. Dark glasses didn't help. A baseball cap to hide his hair only made matters worse.

"Where can we go that I won't be recognized?"

"In Houston? Nowhere. You're the Astros' leading pitcher this season. Your picture is in the paper almost every day. And today we were both featured in the sports section."

"Yes, your mother mentioned that picture."

"It was horrible. I'm surprised the caption didn't read 'Baseball star to wed cross-eyed groupie.' Your fault, of course. I was trying not to throw a *real* tantrum." Stevie was seeing more and more aspects of fame that she didn't like.

"You looked beautiful, as usual. Now help me think of someplace we can shop in peace."

"Impossible. You're a hometown hero. Every kid in Houston who's ever picked up a baseball dreams of becoming you."

"And wants my autograph." Dusty started the car and shifted it into reverse. "Maybe the Galleria. It's usually full of out-of-towners."

"And kids using the ice rink." Stevie sighed. "You're remarkably patient with the kids. That last group was so enthusiastic I was worried, but you eased us out of there in record time and left every one of them happy."

"Hey, when Mike and I were kids, we stood in line for hours for Bob Gibson's autograph. What a pitcher. Then he left before our turn came." Dusty chuckled, the rich sound rumbling through her. "You wouldn't believe what we did then."

"What?" Stevie was mesmerized by the gleam in his eyes, the dimples denting his tanned cheeks.

"We followed Gibson into the men's room."

"Oh, no!"

"Oh, yes." Dusty shook his head and laughed. "He went into a stall. I know why now."

"Hmm?" To heck with colognes. If the cosmetics industry could bottle that laugh, distill the Dusty Derrick charisma into a fragrance for men. . . .

"I've had jerks try to take my picture at a urinal. Can you imagine?" He looked at her and Stevie felt her cheeks go hot. Imagine? If only she couldn't.

"So what about Gibson?"

"We waited until he came out and ambushed him. The guy was a real gentleman. Took a moment to sign gloves for a couple of pushy brats." Dusty cleared his throat. "I never forgot it. Still have that glove too."

"So you indulge all the pushy brats too." It wasn't fair. Now she even admired him. She was going to self-combust soon from all the warm, not to mention hot, thoughts zinging through her. Most settled with unerring accuracy into a certain spot that had her wiggling in her seat. "That's nice, Dusty."

"Well, I try. Now let's get going."

"You'll need a disguise if you really intend to buy me some clothes today."

"Whatever. But I've got to get over to the hospital first. Then you can do your worst."

Stevie grinned.

"There. No one will recognize you now," Stevie said several hours later.

"I guess not." Dusty frowned at the man in the mirror with the shaggy gray-streaked hair. A full beard and matching mustache covered the lower half of his face. "You just added ten years to my age. Where did this stuff come from? This one of your undercover disguises?"

"Of course not. A friend left it here." Stevie wouldn't look at him when she grabbed his chin and picked up a pencil. "Your eyebrows need to be darker. Details are important."

"A boyfriend?" He grabbed her wrist. It felt surprisingly delicate. Stevie seemed so tough, so capable. She finally met his gaze, her dark eyes startled. He forgot for a moment why he was aggravated with her. She licked her lips and he almost pulled her into his lap.

"You told me you were unattached. Who left this stuff?"

Stevie deftly popped his fingers loose. "You're getting personal with the hired help again, Derrick. Sit still and let me do my job." She stroked the pencil across his eyebrows, then turned away to fuss in a small makeup kit.

Getting personal. Dusty realized that if he got as personal with the lady as he wanted, she'd be naked right now and under him. Or maybe over him, her breasts close enough for him to taste. He shifted, impatient with his tendency lately to daydream himself into hardness.

"Huh?" She looked as if he was supposed to do something.

"I said stand up and pull up your shirt."

"Now you're talking." Dusty pulled off his T-shirt and threw it against the wall.

"Behave. I want you to wear this under it. It's going to complete the look. This will be great." She came at him with a long pillow, Velcro straps dangling from it. When she reached around him to fasten it, he pulled her close, his hands on her hips. She felt good, her soft breasts mashed against him.

"I know something else that would be great right now."

Her cheeks were pink, but she frowned and her eyes warned him to quit rushing her.

"Okay, I'll behave." Dusty released her, hoping he didn't imagine a flare of disappointment in her coffee-colored eyes.

"Thanks." Stevie retrieved his shirt. "Put this on over it." She made adjustments, then stepped back. "Take a look."

Dusty stepped up to the full-length mirror on the back of the bathroom door.

"God almighty!"

"You could go anywhere in Houston like this and no one would look twice." She was grinning, so damned sexy it was all he could do not to drag her down the hall to her bedroom. Soon. It was only a matter of time. Most women. . . .

But Stevie wasn't most women. She was an undercover cop. Though why anyone would want to be was a mystery to him. The story she'd told him last night had been enough to scare the hell out of him. Cops were killed in the line of duty all the time. Mike, this Riley partner of hers. You'd think she'd jump at the chance to get away from police work.

Although Stevie was proud of what she did and rightly so. Hell, Dusty couldn't figure it out and Stevie was waiting for him. He looked down at his waistline.

"Did you have to make me middle-aged *and* fat?" He shifted the puffy bulk that hung over his belt. "I look like I've spent the last fifteen years drinking beer and only watching baseball."

"That's why this is so perfect!" Stevie laughed and patted Ranger, who woofed in agreement. "You still look pretty good." She poked at his pretend gut. "If a little soft."

"Soft, huh?" He grabbed her, rubbing his newly whiskered chin across her cheek. "Want me to show you just how hard I am under all this?"

She stepped back, her face fiery. "Cut it out, Dusty."

He let her go reluctantly. Damn, she smelled good, felt good. He had to take his time here. At least he was sure that she would be worth waiting for.

"Let's go. Seeing what it's like to be someone else might be fun. Like what you've been doing for years. You'll have to tell me more about going undercover."

"It's pretty tedious most of the time. I'm sure you have better stories. Like your adventures with Madonna." Stevie marched to the door. "I'll drive. Your car is too recognizable."

"There weren't any adventures. And the vanity

plates weren't my idea." Dusty followed her down the steps to the underground parking garage, admiring the snug fit of her white jeans and the sway of her hips.

"Let me guess. Your agent. Or your publicist. I can't believe he called this morning." Stevie jingled her keys. "I hate all this media attention."

Dusty reached out to squeeze her shoulder when she stopped beside a late model Honda Accord.

"He's been fielding calls all morning about my engagement. I asked him to hold the tabloids off, didn't I?"

"Yes, thank you." Stevie unlocked the car and slid in, stretching across to unlock the passenger door.

Stretching showed off the way she filled out her red tank top. Dusty opened the door. Stevie was built with generous curves. Did she have a bra under the top? Or was she still that high, that firm? He wished he could remember how she'd looked in Cocoa Beach.

Dusty got into the car, grumbling when his knees hit the dashboard. He was sick of relying on old memories, and more than ready to make new ones.

"Slide the seat back." Stevie started the engine and fastened her seat belt. A narrow strap of red satin drooped down one arm and she tucked it efficiently over her shoulder before turning to back out of the parking space.

Dusty adjusted the seat and fastened his own belt. A red satin bra. One of those lace ones with a front clip, he bet. He came near to groaning out loud at the mental picture that gave him. He had to slow down. Stevie wasn't ready. But he was. So damned ready he hurt.

Stevie seemed to think he'd had this wild life in Hollywood. But besides a few staged publicity dates, his life had been relatively quiet, the way he liked it. Dusty opened his mouth to say something that would probably get him in trouble when his cell phone chirped from his pocket.

"Derrick."

"I miss you, Dusty. When are you coming home?"

"Bebe?" Dusty looked at Stevie. She pulled into a convenience store parking lot.

"Sure, honey. It's me. Your number one fan."

"You shouldn't have ruined those clothes, Bebe."

"Why not? That woman doesn't belong in your house. *I* do."

"I told you I get lonely. Meet me for coffee somewhere. How can I connect with you?" Dusty's fingers ached and he realized he was gripping the phone. Stevie was frowning at him and mouthing for him to pick a public place. "How about outside the Dome after the game tomorrow night?"

"Eager, aren't you? New girl not satisfying you?" Bebe laughed. "Not yet, Dusty. Maybe after Sunday's game. You're pitching then, aren't you?"

"That's the plan. Let's make a date. Your notes tell me you know what I like. Maybe I *have* hooked up with the wrong woman." Dusty would have smiled at the look on Stevie's face if he hadn't been wound so tight. Damn this Bebe female. He was going to have to quit answering the phone.

"Oh, Dusty. I could do such things with you, to you, for you. Things that bitch couldn't possibly do." She laughed again. "Break Nolan Ryan's record Sunday and I'll be waiting for you after the game."

"Where—" Bebe had hung up and Dusty slapped the phone shut.

"What did she say?" Stevie grabbed the phone. "Do you have caller return? I don't know why I didn't think of it sooner."

"Yeah. Hit star 69." Dusty watched Stevie punch in numbers. It was obvious after a few moments that Bebe wasn't answering.

"What do you bet she's calling from another pay phone?"

"I'm not betting anything on that lunatic. With luck we can end this Sunday night." Dusty scratched at his face. "I think I'm allergic to this adhesive, Stevie. Let's hurry up and get the shopping done."

Stevie put the car in gear. She *had* to get a grip. She'd actually been jealous when she'd heard Dusty talking to Bebe. Jealous of a stalker? She glanced at Dusty. Even in the disguise he was entirely too sexy. No wonder Bebe had fallen for him.

And Bebe hadn't seen him work his way through the children's ward of the cancer hospital this morning. Seeing Dusty in action as a sports hero had given Stevie a whole new warm spot where he was concerned, this one closer to her heart. No, she couldn't still be in love with Dusty. They were too different. Wanted such different things out of life. He wanted a home, a family. She wanted . . . a home, a family.

The difference was in the details. He would expect a stay-at-home woman, not a wife who ran an anti-drug task force with huge responsibilities. Stevie tried to dredge up some of the enthusiasm for her new job that had had her pumped up for days. She *was* excited about it, damn it.

She steered into the shopping center parking lot. Dusty was her assignment. It was only natural that her entire focus was on him. But she had to ignore this mutual attraction.

He did want her. His eyes devoured her, made her feel hot, sexy, incredible really. Inside the mall, he nudged her toward a fancy lingerie shop.

"Come on, Stephanie Jane. Bebe ruined some of your underwear and you definitely need a nightgown." He grabbed her hand, that twinkle in his eyes warning her he would probably embarrass her in front of some poor saleswoman. Feeling doomed and ridiculously flattered, Stevie let him pull her into the store.

Nine

"What's on the schedule today?" Stevie had quickly learned that Dusty was a busy man. Leisurely days with time for soaking in the spa hadn't happened again in the week since their shopping trip. She'd been relieved that Dusty had quit pressuring her on the marriage issue. They'd settled into a kind of friendly truce, though there was a constant sexual awareness just beneath the surface.

"Lunch at the Hyatt." Dusty tossed a ball for Ranger. The vet declared the dog fit, but had prescribed some eyedrops. Cursing Bebe, Dusty carefully put in the drops on schedule.

"I guess there's no chance that it's just lunch." The Hyatt was a fairly ritzy hotel downtown. Stevie looked down at her usual jeans. Acting the part of Dusty's fiancée had challenged her wardrobe to the max.

"The Astros Wives Club is hosting a fundraising luncheon for the Ronald MacDonald house at the Cancer Center."

"And why are *you* going to a Wives function?" Astros wives were young, beautiful women whose husbands made millions as professional athletes. Women with manicures, designer wardrobes and perfect hair. Her own hair was wild, weeks overdue for a trim. And her nails . . . she crammed them in her jeans pockets.

"I'm, uh, getting an award." Dusty crouched in front of Ranger.

"An award for what?" *Hunk of the Year.* Too trite. *Tightest Tush.* Entirely possible. No, something even sexier. *Man Most Likely to Take Me to the Promised Land.* Stevie felt her cheeks grow warm. The Promised Land had eluded her ever since Cocoa Beach. If she gave in and slept with Dusty would it happen again? Or was there something wrong with her, as her ex-husband had once snidely suggested?

Dusty had quit asking. Maybe he didn't want her anymore. Fine. That's what she'd wanted, wasn't it? So why did she feel like bursting into tears?

"They're honoring me for my work with the Sunshine Kids." Suddenly very busy picking a burr from Ranger's fur, Dusty wouldn't look at her and the back of his neck was red.

"You mean the kids with terminal cancer? Like those we visited the other day?"

"Yeah. I'm a sucker for those thin faces and big eyes." Dusty gave Ranger a final pat and stood. "I'd better go change. These events go on forever, but I'm sure we can slip out before the inevitable fashion show."

"Wait a minute. I have a question." Stevie reached out and touched his arm. He stopped and put his warm hand over hers then slid it above her elbow, under her sleeve. Hmmm. The noise from her body was getting louder every day. Heat, chemistry, whatever you called it, she felt it and forgot everything else when she was near Dusty. She wanted him desperately and not just for sex. She'd caught herself daydreaming a lot lately. Of a life with Dusty. A home with Dusty. A family with Dusty.

Anything with Dusty would be better than anything without him.

"Thanks for being such an asset this week. You've got the role of fiancée down pat." He smiled and squeezed her hand, and might as well have squeezed her heart.

"Are you forgetting the reception at the Petroleum Club?" Stevie looked down. His tanned hand covering her paler one made their contrasts so obvious. Masculine versus feminine. Indoor person, outdoor person. Center stage, backstage. Stevie pulled back, needing distance in more ways than one.

"Anyone can have an accident. I didn't need that Exxon commercial anyway."

"They took back the offer?" Stevie looked up. His dimples gave him away. "Okay, keep pulling my chain, big guy. I wonder what disaster I can cause at this luncheon . . ."

"Do your worst, Stephanie Jane. It wasn't your fault that the oil company exec was trying to swallow a piece of steak when that olive disappeared down your blouse. You saved the day with the Heimlich maneuver. I was proud to call you mine."

Stevie grabbed Ranger's collar, her knees suddenly wobbly. Dusty's compliments meant entirely too much to her. He was much too easy to love.

"Don't say I didn't warn you. Now what did you do besides visit those kids to win an award?" Stevie let go of Ranger and followed Dusty to the back door.

He pulled open the back door, then stopped to grin sheepishly over his shoulder, "I built them a camp."

* * *

Stevie settled into the passenger seat of the Ferrari and tugged down her skirt. She loved the expensive suit she wore, one Dusty had insisted she buy during their shopping spree. The white silk skirt was a tad too short, but Dusty had complimented her legs. Okay, so she wasn't immune to a little flattery. Especially since they'd probably be trailed by the inevitable horde of photographers today.

Dusty's agent had tried to hold off the tabloids, but the story was too hot. She and Dusty were hounded whenever they appeared in public. Her picture would probably be taken at least a dozen times today.

"You look great, Stevie." Dusty grinned and steered the car out of his neighborhood and onto the freeway toward downtown Houston.

"Thanks. You look pretty fine yourself." He did look especially handsome in his very expensive and very Italian gray suit. A blue and yellow tie and white shirt brought out his tan and the color of his eyes. Stevie realized she was staring. Was there an award for Most Beautiful Man?

"Where is this camp you built?"

"In the hill country. Near Austin. There's a lake, cabins, the usual camp stuff, plus a first-class medical facility."

Stevie mentally calculated what it must have cost and whistled. "Pretty generous."

"Hey, I can afford it." He slipped on dark glasses and cleared his throat. "And I've been damned lucky all my life."

Stevie reached over to squeeze his hand on the steering wheel. "My hero."

"Okay, okay. Knock it off. Now let me warn you about the Astros Wives."

"Warn me? Are they dangerous?" Stevie hid her

hands in her lap. Cream and clear polish had done little to erase the impression that she dug turnips for a living. Dangerous wives . . . she liked the concept.

"You may think so. I'm sure they'll try to ambush you when we get there. Try to recruit you for their committees at the very least. As my fiancée, you're fresh meat."

"Great." He just wouldn't look at her. Maybe he was finally realizing what he'd done with his announcement. Or wondering if she would embarrass him. Stevie stiffened, reassuring herself that she could hold her own with anybody, especially with women who had just happened to marry well.

She quickly deflated. Wives were one thing, but the parents were another . . . his parents, her parents. His mother had called three times with wedding questions. Her mother called daily. And his publicist had even asked if Stevie had any glamour shots for him to send out—preferably with her in some barely-there dress. Glamorous she'd never been. It was so obvious that she wasn't right for Dusty.

"It never stops, does it?" Stevie couldn't wiggle her toes in her high-heeled pumps. They were worthless for walking, but she had to look the part.

"You get used to it." Dusty exited the freeway and downshifted to stop at a light.

"I wonder if Bebe will be there."

"Bebe? I doubt it." He steered into the parking garage of the large hotel. "She's never let me see her yet. I can't imagine she'd want to approach me at such a public event." He smiled ruefully. "If she does, the photographers will have a field day."

"If she does, I'll have her in handcuffs before you can say flashbulb." Stevie hoped she wasn't lying. She rubbed her purse, unfashionably bulky because of the gun inside.

"Be careful, Stephanie Jane. I have plans for you." Dusty pulled up to the entrance and a valet ran up to open Stevie's door. Stevie slid out, her face hot again. Plans? How about an amorous romp on his king-size waterbed, complete with champagne? She looked up at the hotel. Or a honeymoon suite right here?

Before she could stop them, Dusty and the attendant drove off, leaving her standing at the hotel entrance. A few minutes later, Dusty strolled up, slipping his keys and his sunglasses into his pants pocket.

"Why'd you do that? I'm supposed to be with you at all times." Stevie let him take her elbow and lead her into the massive lobby with a thirty-story atrium.

"I was gone less than five minutes. And did you see that kid's face? If I'd just handed over the keys to the Ferrari, he'd be halfway to Mexico by now."

"Just don't disappear on me again, okay?" Stevie pasted a smile on her face and walked beside him to the escalator. There was a mob—if you could call a gathering of the bold and the beautiful a mob—heading down to the main ballroom. Stevie's stomach descended along with the escalator. She didn't belong here. Even worse, photographers trapped them on the lower level. Stevie kept her brilliant smile and pressed herself against Dusty's side.

"You look great. I mean it, I'm proud to call you mine," Dusty whispered.

"Oh, swell, no pressure there." She gripped his forearm, reassured by how solid he felt. The photographers soon moved on to snap a female TV news anchor. "My hair's wild, my skirt is definitely too short . . ."

"I like you wild and short skirts show off your long

legs. I have fantasies about those legs, you know." He steered her to a table set up in the doorway of the ballroom. A woman in a hot-pink suit leapt to her feet, insisting on personally showing them to the head table.

Stevie drifted along at his side in something of a haze, imagining her legs in all sorts of interesting positions. She had to come back down to earth. Dusty's compliments meant entirely too much to her.

Women stopped to gawk openly at the beautiful man at her side. He totally ignored them, pausing at the table to smile into her eyes, into ordinary Stephanie Jane Powell's eyes, with such pride and affection that she wanted to pull his face down to kiss him until they were both breathless. She was ridiculously close to tears, her heart expanding until her clothes felt too tight.

They settled into seats facing a sea of tables while silent waiters filled their water glasses and brought fancy salads with what looked like weeds and mandarin oranges.

"Thanks, Stevie," Dusty whispered. "You're fantastic."

Stevie sipped and chewed and sipped some more, in the throes of some kind of emotional overload. She really loved Dusty, loved his kindness, loved watching his hands as he forked up salad and slathered a crusty roll with butter. Loved the way his eyes crinkled when he grinned at her commentary on the mystery chicken dish they were served next. She even loved the way he slipped his hand under her napkin to stroke her knee when the mistress of ceremonies began to introduce him.

The introduction was another revelation. Dusty had not only built and furnished a camp, he'd spent countless hours there in the off-season teaching groups of kids the basics of baseball. His acceptance speech was just the right blend of humility and a pitch for more money and volunteers to help the Sunshine Kids. The large crowd, mostly women, gave him a standing ovation.

"We'll leave as soon as you're through with dessert," he murmured when a break was announced before a fashion show could begin. Stevie glanced at her barely touched chocolate mousse. She'd lost her appetite along with her heart. She was dazzled and on the verge of doing something momentous.

"I'm through. Just let me go to the ladies' room first." Stevie dropped her napkin on her chair and left him to work her way to the doorway on the other side of the ballroom.

"Ms. Powell, may I have a moment?" Stevie stopped beside a well-dressed woman in her early thirties. "I'm Cindy Benson, Tom's wife. You know, Dusty's catcher?"

"Sure." Stevie smiled and extended her hand. "Nice to meet you. Dusty raves about Tom."

"And vice versa. It's so good to finally meet you." Cindy grabbed Stevie's elbow to steer her to an empty space near the rest room door. "There's a line in there. Why don't you give me a minute to twist your arm?" Cindy grinned, thoroughly charming and obviously very determined.

Stevie snatched back her hand with a laugh. "Dusty warned me about this. I'm not a wife yet."

Cindy laughed. "A formality. I tell you, Tom's mourning Dusty's bachelorhood. I think he was living vicariously through him. And I'm in awe. How'd you get that guy to commit?"

"You could say I was in the right place at the right

time." Stevie's smile twitched. "When Dusty was ready to settle down, he acted fast and I was there."

"He told Tom you were childhood sweethearts."

"Something like that."

"That's so romantic." Cindy sighed, looking wistful for a moment. "Now, down to business. I don't know what Dusty's told you about the Astros Wives Club, but we need you, Stevie. We work for some very special causes." Cindy gripped Stevie's arm. "The Sunshine Kids is just one of them."

"Oh, don't worry, Cindy. I know my role in Dusty's life." Stevie eased away. If she kept reminding herself that she was only his bodyguard, maybe it would help. "We'll talk. I promise. But I really, really need to go to the bathroom." Lights flashed. "And, look, the show's starting."

Cindy scurried back to the head table while Stevie hurried into the bathroom, which, fortunately, was empty. She slipped into a stall and latched the door. Ah, relief. She was tugging up her pantyhose when there was a bang on the stall door.

"I'll be right out."

"Don't bother, missy." The husky voice echoed in the small room and was unfortunately familiar.

"Bebe?" Stevie quickly jerked down her skirt and slipped open the lock. She tried to shove the heavy wood door open, but it wouldn't budge. Damn, she'd left her purse hooked on the back of her chair. What had she been thinking? Now here she was with a chance to end this and no real weapon. Tossing a roll of toilet paper at the lady wouldn't exactly discourage her.

"What's going on, Bebe?" Stevie heard a weird laugh.

"You just won't leave him alone, will you? I warned you what would happen."

Stevie realized that the stall walls and door went almost to the ceiling and to less than a foot from the marble floor. She looked down, but all she could see were red pumps, then a trash can sliding across the floor. She banged on the solid door, even tried a kick that snapped off a heel.

"What are you doing, Bebe?"

"Taking care of the competition, sugar." There was a whoosh and Stevie smelled smoke.

"This is crazy. There are smoke detectors, a sprinkler system—"

"Crazy? You think I'm crazy?" The voice rose and there was a hard thump on the door. "Shut up and say your prayers." The outer door slammed and Stevie realized she was alone.

"Damn!" Stevie hit the door again, then stepped out of her shoes and wiggled her tight skirt up to her waist. Smoke drifted down, making her eyes water and her throat raw. She coughed and got down on her knees, rolling over onto her back to try to slide under the stall and out.

With a welcome screech, the smoke detectors came to life and sprinklers began to spray Stevie with cool water. She turned her head and began scooting under the door, wishing she'd thought to pull off her jacket first.

"Stevie!" The door crashed open and two large feet in black Gucci loafers slid to a stop near her nose. "Fire!"

Stevie heard water running, crashes, bangs and curses. She was busy squashing her boobs flat enough to clear the door. Finally, she slid free and into Dusty's arms. Water continued to pour from the sprinklers in the ceiling and she wiped at her face. A trash can smoldered nearby. The smoke was thick but clearing, drifting out the open door. Stevie coughed and staggered out of the room with Dusty's arms around her.

"God, Stevie, you okay?"

Stevie gasped when they came into the relatively fresh air in the chaotic ballroom. Ceiling sprinklers, obviously on the same circuit as the restroom, dutifully drizzled the room and everyone in it. If she hadn't been so sick, so mad and so ashamed, Stevie would have laughed at the sight of the beautiful people wailing their misery at being drenched.

She hugged Dusty, pulling her purse from where it hung ridiculously from his shoulder. She couldn't speak, could only gasp for breath and hold onto him.

"What the hell happened?" he asked against her wet hair.

"Bebe," she managed to croak before coughing again. Cindy appeared and handed Stevie a glass of water.

"I can't believe it!" Cindy cried. "I heard the trash can in the bathroom caught fire. What do you bet someone was smoking in there?" Cindy patted Stevie's back. "Are you okay? Did the stall door stick?"

"I'm taking her to a doctor, Cindy." Dusty saw hotel personnel with fire extinguishers rush into the bathroom. The fire alarms stopped and the sprinklers slowed to a trickle.

"This is terrible," Cindy said, following them to the door. "I hope no one demands a refund. They ate lunch after all." Dusty looked at Cindy with new admiration. Her designer suit was soaked, her hundred-dollar hair plastered to her head and her makeup had made black streaks on her cheeks. Yet the woman was worried about refunds.

"Remind them it's for charity, Cindy."

"Oh, I will. And don't let this discourage you, Stevie. I'll call you later in the week."

Dusty hustled Stevie, who was unusually quiet, out of the room through a side door. "I'm sure as hell not letting photographers get a crack at us," he muttered, whisking her out of the hotel and into the car. Damn it, he was still shaking. Stevie in a burning bathroom. He'd never been so scared in his life. Not even when he'd almost lost his pitching arm in a freak boating accident as a teenager. Stevie could have died.

He carefully buckled her in, smoothing her wet hair back from her pale forehead. He'd hired her to come between him and his stalker, but the life and death risk just hadn't been real to him. He started to speak and had to clear his throat.

"Stevie honey, are you all right? Can you talk?"

"Yes," Stevie rasped. "Can we just go home? Please?"

"But you need a doctor. All that smoke . . ."

She reached up and squeezed his hand. "I'm all right. Please. I just want to go home."

He looked at her carefully. She seemed to be breathing easier and was definitely one of the sexiest drowned rats he'd ever seen. Her red top was plastered to her like a second skin. Sexy? To hell with that. If he'd lost her . . .

"You sure?" She nodded. "If you feel the least bit woozy, we're going to the emergency room." He slammed the door and went around to get in on the driver's side. Stevie rested her head on the back of the seat, her eyes closed, her purse clutched in her lap. Her purse, with that damned gun. Stevie really was a cop. He hated the idea. Had to figure out a way—

To what? To save her? She wouldn't thank him for

that. She'd already made it clear she wasn't about to give up her job.

"You haven't passed out, have you?"

"No." She opened one bloodshot eye. "Quit nagging me and drive. Please?"

She hadn't coughed again and had more color in her cheeks.

"You win." He drove, but he wanted answers. This couldn't go on. His heart had almost stopped when he'd heard the fire alarm. He'd been standing by the ladies' room door waiting for Stevie so they could make a quick getaway. He'd seen a woman come out and then—

He smacked his hand on the steering wheel and Stevie jumped. She stared at him with red-rimmed eyes.

"What?"

"I saw Bebe."

Ten

Stevie spent a long time in the shower, soaping and shampooing away the smoke that had seeped into her pores. She spent more time blowing her hair dry, stalling. She couldn't face Dusty. When he knocked on her locked bedroom door for the third time to check on her, she reluctantly opened it.

"Are you okay?" He was obviously concerned.

"I'll live." She was being churlish. She dredged up a smile. "Thanks for asking."

His frown deepened. "Come out to the den." He turned and strode down the hall.

"Dusty, we need to—" Stevie stopped when she realized Dusty wasn't alone. "What's *he* doing here?"

"I called him."

"You're firing me." Stevie nodded at Mac and sank down on the other end of the forest green leather sofa.

"Damn right I am." Dusty didn't sit. Instead he paced the jewel-toned Oriental rug in front of the fireplace, dragging his hand through his hair. "Tell her, Mac."

"Dusty wants you pulled off the case." Mac looked like he'd just come from yet another police funeral. He had on the formal uniform decorated with his commendation and his rank. He obviously wasn't happy and Stevie knew why.

"I deserve it. I totally failed Dusty. Thank God, Bebe went after me today and not him, because I totally lost my focus."

"I don't want to discuss it. Just pack up and get out." Dusty turned his back to stare into the empty fireplace.

Tears filled her eyes. She wanted to go to him, to touch his rigid back and beg his forgiveness. No, she didn't deserve it. She'd failed him, risked his life because she'd let emotion destroy her concentration. "Who'll watch you?"

Dusty turned and stared at her. "Mac can get me somebody. I can tolerate a man for a day or two. If Bebe makes good on her promise to meet me Sunday, we should be able to wrap this up then."

"A man? But you didn't want—"

"Let it go, Stevie. I want you off the case. Go pack."

Stevie searched for the tenderness she usually saw in Dusty's face. Nothing. Only a stern set to his jaw that told her he was really angry. She deserved it, but it still hurt. One mistake and she was history? What about the marriage talk? She slumped in her seat.

"Okay, you're the boss."

"No, I am." Mac finally spoke, leaning forward, his hands on his knees. "Stevie's not going anywhere."

"But, Mac—" Stevie's protest mingled with Dusty's and they both stared at Mac.

"Stevie, I want to hear exactly what happened." Mac looked at Dusty. "Why don't you leave us alone and let us hash this out. If Stevie deserves an official reprimand . . ."

"No! She's been on vacation, remember? You can't use this on her record." Dusty sat on the stone ledge surrounding the fireplace. "I just want her off this case, that's all."

"Let me talk to Mac, Dusty. This is police business." Stevie tossed her hair back over her shoulder and turned to face her boss. "I deserve a reprimand, a demotion, some kind of punishment. I was inches away from the stalker, Mac, and I let her get away." Stevie held her shaking hands together.

"She was so close to Dusty, he actually saw her. My God. She could have . . ." Stevie's throat clogged with tears.

"Relax, Stevie. We'll sort this out." Mac put a hand on her shoulder. "Dusty, what did she look like? Still blond? Does she look like the photos we have?"

"Hell, I was watching for Stevie, not some nutcase." Dusty rubbed his forehead. "Had on red, I think. Tall, similar to the pictures but. . . . Oh, I don't know."

"You hear that, Mac? She was wearing red and I didn't even notice her." Stevie jumped up. "I'll pack right now. There's no way I can continue this. I'm absolutely worthless to Dusty."

"Sit down, Stevie." Mac made his order firm and Stevie sat. Her stomach was in knots. She was sick with disappointment. Dusty must be eager to get rid of her. What about those marriage proposals? Too late. Besides failing him she'd turned him down over and over again. He was obviously fed up. With her, with them.

"Dusty, let us discuss this. Alone, please. Go play with your dog or something."

Dusty stood and jammed his hands in his pockets. He'd changed into shorts and a T-shirt and even frowning looked so good Stevie felt close to tears. Not quiet little pitiful tears either, but big, noisy sobs. This was a great time to realize she loved him and would do anything to be his, she thought bitterly.

"I'll go work out in the weight room, but hear me, Mac. I want Stevie out of here tonight. If you think I still need someone, send over some palooka, but Stevie goes." He turned on his heel and in moments Stevie heard the back door slam as he headed for his weight room attached to the garage.

"You shut the gate when you came in, didn't you?" Stevie asked anxiously, images of Bebe with a blowtorch bringing her to her feet. Was the woman partial to fire? Would she and Dusty wind up fried in their beds some night? No, hold it. There was no "she and Dusty." She was leaving.

"He'll be okay. I've got a detail sitting right outside the gate." Mac smiled for the first time since she'd come into the room. "Now give me your report, Detective. What exactly happened at the Hyatt today?"

Stevie forced herself to give a dispassionate account. But when she was finally finished, she had to hug herself, chilled by the hatred Bebe had felt for her.

"Bebe was there, Mac. And I let her get the best of me. While I was struggling to get out, she could have hurt Dusty, done whatever she wanted and I couldn't have stopped her." Stevie angrily swiped at a tear. "I didn't even remember to take my gun into the bathroom!"

Mac cleared his throat. "I don't know, Stevie. It was unrealistic to think that one person could take care of Dusty twenty-four hours a day. Hell, everybody needs to take a leak occasionally."

"You don't understand!" Stevie jumped up and stared down at Mac. "Dusty is right to blame me. I failed him. I was so into him, so wrapped up in him personally I didn't give a single thought to his safety. I will never forgive myself for that." She took a deep breath. "If Dusty hadn't beat me to it, I would have definitely taken myself off the case."

Mac sat for a long moment then shook his head. "No matter what Dusty wants, it's too late to get anyone else in and bring them up to speed. You've got to put whatever personal feelings you have aside and just do this."

"I . . . I can't," Stevie whispered, looking down at her bare feet. She'd forgotten to put on shoes. And she'd left her ruined high heels in the Hyatt bathroom stall. She had totally lost her concentration. And all because she'd fallen for Dusty. Hard. So hard she felt like she'd been dropped on her head, not merely smoked and drenched today.

"Okay, you forgot your gun. Bebe got the best of you." Mac sat back. "You've snapped back from worse situations."

"It's not the situation. It's . . . it's Dusty." Stevie blinked back her tears.

"Is he giving you a hard time? Making you uncomfortable?" Mac leaned forward. "He's my friend but if he's doing anything—"

"No!" Stevie sank down on the couch. "I love him."

"So? I'd say that was handy since you're engaged to him."

"Mac!" Stevie jumped up again. "I've lost my objectivity. You know this engagement is phony. And so how can I protect him when I'm half-crazy in love with him?"

Mac pulled out a handkerchief and handed it to Stevie. "Damn, Stevie. You sure know how to complicate things. Sit down and wipe your eyes."

Stevie stared at him. He was so calm. Couldn't he see how impossible this was? He patted the seat beside him again and she sat, mopping her face.

"Today we saw that Bebe can be dangerous. Right?" Mac picked up a notebook and flipped it open.

"Right. Trapping me in the toilet stall when I was alone. What a rookie mistake. That's why I've got to pull out of this."

"My report says the stall door was jammed with a dinner knife. You were in a hotel ballroom with hundreds of other women around. Pure luck that she was able to get you alone." Mac tapped the book with a pen. "I'd say she did this on impulse, no trap to it."

"So what other impulses will she have?" Stevie blew her nose, determined to shut off the waterworks. "I didn't do my job, Mac. Dusty should fire me."

"Dusty's firing you because he's scared to death you'll get hurt."

Stevie pressed the handkerchief to her mouth. Of course, why hadn't she seen it? He thought he loved her, though God knew why. "But—"

"No buts. Bebe walked out of that bathroom and right past him without doing or saying anything. Don't you see, Stevie? Bebe isn't dangerous to Dusty. She's dangerous to you." Mac patted her on the shoulder. "You've managed to deflect her. You get out of the way and she'll hone in on Dusty again. Maybe get mad at him over something and take action. She might even play cat and mouse with him until the end of baseball season and beyond."

"Okay, I see your point." Stevie took a shaky breath, coughing when her lungs reminded her they'd had a rough day. "But my feelings . . ."

"I'm glad you and Dusty are getting along. I couldn't ask for a better woman for my old friend. And from the way he looks at you, this engagement is about as phony as your hair color."

Stevie felt her lips curve in her first smile in hours.

"Be careful, boss. This may look natural, but you never know."

Mac put his arm around her and gave her a quick hug. "I know, Detective. Now quit beating yourself up. Today's incident was your wake-up call. From now on, you keep your eyes open when you're out in public." Mac stood and moved toward the back door. "And actually, Detective Powell, I'd say the closer you are to the man, the better you can guard him."

"I'll take that as an order, sir." Stevie followed him to the door.

"I'm going to let you tell him why you're staying on." Mac stopped and slapped on his cap. "I'm going home and get out of this monkey suit and drink a cold beer."

"Another funeral today?" Stevie reached out and straightened his tie.

"No, thank God. Just an appearance before City Council. Politics." He patted her hand. "Your task force went over big. I'm looking for great things there, Stevie."

"Thanks, boss. I promise I won't let you down." Stevie swiped at yet another tear.

Mac cleared his throat. "Don't let yourself down, Stevie. Bebe's mad at you, not Dusty. There's a detail right outside the gate. Every time you leave here, I'm having you tailed for backup. Bebe's fire didn't hurt anybody much, but it shows definite homicidal tendencies." He opened the door. "Watch your back, Stevie."

Stevie sat back and stared at the ceiling fan revolving above her head. She could still smell smoke, even with her ruined suit in a securely sealed garbage bag in her bathroom.

She was exhausted and had a headache, and still

woozy from her adventure. She didn't dare tell Dusty or she'd end up in the emergency room. She pushed herself up and headed to the bathroom for a couple of aspirin.

"You're not packing."

Stevie jumped, scattering close to a hundred tablets around the bathroom.

"God, you startled me." She got down on her hands and knees and began picking them up.

"Leave them and come to the den. I want to know why Mac's gone and you're not." Dusty grabbed her elbow and marched her into the den. He gently shoved her into a chair. "Wait here." He returned in moments with a can of cold diet soda.

"Thanks, how did you know?" Stevie sipped gratefully.

"You're not as tough as you like to pretend, Stephanie Jane. You wince every time you swallow and you still sound like a female bullfrog." He sat down across from her.

"You're being pretty nice considering you just fired me." Stevie smiled and looked at him through her lashes. Dusty was relieved to see her looking so well and acting sassy again.

"I feel guilty. Bebe hates you because I shot off my mouth."

"I guess I could say 'I told you so.' "

Dusty jumped up and went to crouch in front of her. He took the soda can and set it on the side table, then took her hands in his.

"I'm sorry, Stevie. I was so sure I knew what to do, I didn't listen to someone who knew better. You."

She smiled and squeezed his hands. "At last you get it. I *am* the expert in these kinds of situations. If you'd listened to me—" She stopped and turned a becoming pink. "Hey, I've got no right to lecture you. This expert let a stalker make a fool out of her and put you in danger. I'm not fit to guard your body."

"I didn't say that. It's just—" Dusty pulled her close and rested his chin on her hair. Damn, it still smelled like strawberries after all these years. He ran his hands over the curve of her hips, leaned closer to her wonderfully full breasts. He loved the feel of her. She was all woman. He needed for her to be all his.

"Honey, you scared the hell out of me. When I realized you were trapped in a burning room . . ."

"You can't fire me, Dusty," she murmured, snuggling closer and wrapping her arms around his waist.

"The hell I can't." He pried her arms off of him. "This job is over. I will not—"

"What?" She frowned up at him. "Not risk me again? Sorry, love, but I'm seeing this through until the end. Mac's providing some back-up and I'm sure we can wrap this up on Sunday."

"I don't like it, Stevie."

"Like it or not, it's a done deal. Now why don't we figure out some way to make the best of it?"

Eleven

"Bebe's been unusually quiet since the Hyatt." Stevie rotated her neck, jumping when Dusty moved up behind her and began to massage her tight muscles.

"So have you. You fell asleep on the couch last night before I could make my move." Dusty's hands were magic, kneading the tension out of her neck and shoulders.

"Mmmm . . . you're awfully good at that." She shifted forward to let his hands move down her back. "You mean I missed your move? I guess the excitement took more out of me than I realized." They were in Dusty's den, Ranger at their feet, after the Astros had won an afternoon game. It was Saturday night. Tomorrow Dusty would pitch and, with luck, Bebe would meet him and they could end this.

Never see Dusty again? She couldn't imagine it. How did he become so important to her so soon? Soon? Was fifteen years soon?

"Feeling better now?" Dusty's thumbs moved to the base of her spine, sliding under the waistband of her slacks.

"Better? Keep touching me like that and . . ." She moaned a little when he hit a sensitive spot.

"I plan to keep touching you. Everywhere." His breath was against her hair, his hands roving over her stomach.

Stevie was tempted to put his hands exactly where she wanted them, but decided that anticipation would be half the fun. His thumb brushed the underside of her breast.

"Mmmm. That's a nice place to start."

"I've been patient all week, haven't I?" he said, his fingers sliding upward. "Are you going to tell me no?"

Her aching nipples strained against a sheer leopard print bra Dusty had bought for her during their shopping trip. She'd put it on this afternoon, feeling wicked and sexy, imagining what Dusty would say if he could see how it fit, how it plunged.

She was sick of saying no. Sure, she was on duty, but here, surrounded by security. . . . His mouth brushed her ear and she shivered. God, she wanted him.

"No."

"Does that mean yes?" His hands slid up until his thumbs circled her nipples. She turned her head to let his lips work closer to her mouth.

"It means shut up and kiss me."

"Thank God." He turned her and pulled her up against him. She wrapped her arms around him, reveling in his strength. She wasn't exactly little, but he made her feel small, protected.

Suddenly wild for him, she opened her mouth under his. This was more than lust. She knew it, felt it in her heart.

She needed Dusty, needed to touch him. She slid her hands under his shirt to his smooth, warm skin. He stripped off her T-shirt, tossing it across the room, then went still when he saw her leopard print bra.

"You are so beautiful, Stephanie Jane."

Stevie pulled off his shirt and ran her hands up over his rib cage. "So are you."

Suddenly, their hands were feverish, unbuttoning, unzipping until they collapsed on his king-sized waterbed. Dusty touched and tasted her until Stevie begged him to take her, take away the delicious agony of wanting him . . . needing him. He rolled her on top of him, murmuring encouragement when she explored him. He really was beautiful, sleek and muscular.

Dusty fumbled in a drawer and then they were together, gloriously, fitting so perfectly Stevie was thrilled all over again. When he began to move, thought became impossible until she was driven wildly, completely over the edge, holding on to Dusty for dear life. Collapsed on top of him, Stevie rested against his sweat-slicked chest, listening to his thudding heart. Her breathing was as harsh as his was as they came back to earth.

"I'm sorry, Stevie."

Her head snapped up. "Sorry?"

"I meant to make it last."

Stevie snuggled against him. "If it had lasted any longer, I'd be in need of paramedics." A chuckle rumbled through him.

"At least this time I got to see you." He rolled her under him, his eyes bright as he pushed her hair back from her face, then leaned down to kiss each breast. Stevie quivered. So soon. Could she really want him again so soon?

He nodded toward the lamp burning on the bedside table. "From what I remember, our first time we barely had moonlight. I always wished I could have seen your face."

"Just my face?" she teased.

"That and other things." He leaned down to pull a nipple into his mouth until she made little whimpering sounds so totally unlike herself she almost pushed him away.

Instead, she ran her hands down his back and around to his stomach. He jumped and snorted when she brushed his sides.

"You're not going to tickle me, are you? I guarantee it won't turn me on."

"Oh? What does turn you on, Mr. Derrick?"

"Smarty-pants female bodyguards." He grinned and trapped her hands when she tried to touch his sides again. "Behave."

"I don't think you really want me to behave, do you?" His answer was to begin trailing kisses around her navel. Stevie closed her eyes and savored the moment. To have this man want her so much was heady stuff.

"Wait a minute." She tugged at his hair until he looked up at her. "You don't remember our first time?"

He grinned and her heart did a back flip. He was so handsome, so dear.

"Truth?"

"Yes." Stevie traced his ear, fascinated by every part of him. She felt him shudder and smiled. "Did you really do all that in your sleep?"

"Sort of. I'd had pain pills for my shoulder. Everything was hazy the next day. I hope I did right by you. As a virgin, I mean."

Stevie quit smiling. "You were a wonderful lover, Dusty. I pulled a dumb stunt and I was so incredibly lucky—"

"No, I was lucky that you picked me." Dusty kissed

a path down her stomach again, then lower. Oh, God, such exquisite torture.

She begged shamelessly for more, trembling when he loved her with his own wickedly clever mouth. Finally she had to slide down his body to show him how clever she could be. She loved him, every blessed inch of him.

He continued to touch her, his mouth leaving a trail of heat wherever it touched. The back of her knees, the hollow near the end of her spine. Unpredictable places that made her quiver with wild need and call his name.

He took her from one shattering climax to another, leaving her dazed and breathless.

It had been fifteen years since Cocoa Beach. Stevie realized that the few men since Dusty had been rank amateurs. Her husband certainly hadn't known how to touch her there and, oh God, there. With his hands, with his mouth. Stevie sobbed her release, a virgin again for Dusty. . . .

Sunlight woke her. Sunlight and a warm, callused hand roving over her. Stevie sighed and stretched. God, how she loved him. She should tell him. But then she opened her eyes and caught him staring down at her, so seriously it scared her. What was he thinking? He'd asked her to marry him once. Dear God, if he asked her now . . .

No. She couldn't deal with it now. Not with Bebe still out there. When he started to speak, she pulled his head down for an open-mouthed kiss. *Feel, just feel.*

"Stevie, we need to talk."

"After the game, Dusty. After we catch Bebe." Stevie

wouldn't look at him. She was too busy packing, so sure they were going to wrap this up tonight.

"Damn it. Will you quit that?" Dusty grabbed the panties she'd been about to stuff into her suitcase.

"I don't have much time." She plucked the panties from his hand and tossed them into the case and slammed the lid. "Last night shouldn't have happened. It was unprofessional of me. I forgot—" Dusty put a hand over her lips.

"We both forgot. Forgot this damned Bebe thing. Forgot everything but each other. You know why?"

Stevie shook her head, blinking back the tears he could see filling her eyes.

"Because we love each other."

Stevie grabbed his hand and stepped back. "This is crazy. You can't love me, Dusty. You don't really know me."

She was shaking. Dusty reached for her but she backed away, putting the bed between them.

"Why can't you just accept this? Maybe the instinct that drew you to me all those years ago was right."

"Too much has happened since then, Dusty. I was only eighteen, I had a bad case of hero worship and acted on it." She sniffed and swiped at her eyes. "And just because we have great sex together doesn't mean it's love."

"Was last night just sex?" Dusty's hands fell to his sides. He was sick of asking Stevie for something she obviously couldn't or didn't want to give.

"Don't let me keep you then, Ms. Powell. Oh, excuse me, that's Detective Powell, isn't it? I'm due at the ballpark. See you there."

He stormed out of the room, his shoulders stiff.

"Wait!"

He stopped and looked back. "You have something else to say?"

"You can't go without me. It's my job to protect you."

"Right. Sorry, dumb jocks sometimes forget things like that. Grab your gun and let's go then. Wouldn't want to keep Bebe waiting. With luck you can wrap this up tonight and we can both move on with our lives. Thanks for the roll in the hay, it was memorable. I'll be in the car."

He walked down the hall. Stevie heard him order Ranger to stay inside, then shut the door. Memorable? It had been the most wonderful night of her life. What had she done? She loved him. He said he loved her. Why couldn't she just accept the fact that they belonged together? Accept and turn herself into the kind of woman he needed in his life? Flitting around with the Astros Wives, doing good deeds in between carpools and bake sales?

She picked up her purse, the weight reminding her she did indeed have her gun and was ready and able to use it. *Oh, Dusty, we're too different.* She grabbed a tissue and mopped her face before going out to meet him.

"Hasn't Dusty bought you a ring yet?" His mom.

"Are you going to wear white?" Her mom.

"Only three more strikeouts and that record's in the bag." His dad.

"Why so blue, pumpkin?" Her dad.

Stevie forced a smile. "Just worried about Dusty, Dad. This record means a lot to him."

"Sure does." Dusty's dad patted her shoulder.

"Damn, Adam, if our kids aren't perfect together. Imagine the grandkids?"

Stevie scanned the crowd, trying to tune out the foursome around her. Was Bebe here? Maybe even close enough to hear the family conversation? She wouldn't like the topics. Wedding plans. Grandchildren. Stevie's heart felt bruised. She wanted those things. And with Dusty. But it was so hard to imagine how it could work. He was a superstar, worth millions. She was a cop with too many credit cards and a monster mortgage on her condo.

Was she stupid for not jumping at the chance to live what most women would consider a fantasy life? She and Dusty did need to talk. After the game. After Bebe. Eager to finish this, Stevie turned to scan the crowd. Where was Bebe? She saw a sea of faces, part of a standing-room-only crowd hoping to see Dusty break the strikeout record. This was impossible.

A wild cheer erupted. Another batter fanned out. The parents jumped up, screaming and waving. Stevie did the same, aware of her father's worried gaze.

"Go, Dusty!" she shrieked, watching Dusty's face harden as he studied the new batter in front of him. He shook his head at the catcher, finally nodding and starting his wind-up. He looked so powerful, tall and invincible. Stevie had to remind her heart to beat, but she held her breath. The whole crowd was standing.

"Two more outs to go. If Dusty fans them both . . ." Mr. Derrick sniffed. "I'm so damned proud of that boy."

Stevie wiped at her suddenly wet cheeks. Her father tucked a tissue into her clenched fist.

"Relax, pumpkin. He'll do it."

The huge crowd was silent, holding their breaths as Dusty released the ball. There was a crack, a broken bat flying one way, the ball a blur aimed straight at Dusty. It bounced off his shoulder into the first baseman's glove, but Dusty went down.

The crowd screamed its fear, its horror. Players, coaches and trainers ran to surround Dusty who lay unmoving on the dirt of the pitcher's mound.

"What happened?" Stevie clutched Dusty's father's arm, afraid she might throw up.

"Bat was corked. Did you see it fly apart? That ball hit Dusty like a damned missile. We've got to get down there."

"Wait! He's up." The crowd cheered wildly. Dusty was on his feet, waving his cap toward them with his right hand. But his left arm, his golden arm, was wrapped around his body and two trainers hovered around him as he walked off the pitcher's mound and toward the dugout.

The crowd cried out when it became obvious that a new pitcher was warming up and Dusty was leaving the field. An announcer promised an update on Dusty's condition. Stevie swayed on her feet, grateful for her father's arm around her. She sobbed then began pushing her way to the nearest aisle.

"Dusty." Stevie and the parents ran out of the stands to the private elevator down to the players' quarters. Guards kept them outside. Now security worked. She wanted to see Dusty, to be able to comfort him, hold him. He was in with the team doctor, getting x-rays, a solemn-faced trainer told them.

Stevie felt sick, desperate to see him, to reassure him . . . of what? That she loved him? That she wanted to be with him, damn the complications? She paced, his father cursed, both their mothers cried. Stevie's father brought everyone coffee from somewhere while time stood still.

After what seemed like hours but was really only minutes, Dusty appeared in the doorway. Before any of the family could move, shouting reporters surrounded him. Stevie stood on tiptoe to catch a glimpse of him. He looked tired, his arm in a sling, and there were lines of pain and tension in his weary face.

"Dusty!" reporters called. "How bad is it?"

Dusty looked over at his parents, met his father's eyes and shook his head. Then he cleared his throat.

"I'm afraid this is it for me. The ball tore my rotator cuff loose again and the doctor had warned me . . ." He shook his head again, holding up his good hand for silence when there was another burst of questions.

"I'm through. Somebody else can break Nolan Ryan's record. I've had a great career and I'm really sorry to let the team down like this, but my age and injuries have finally caught up with me." He rubbed his forehead with his good hand and looked at Stevie.

"Now I plan to concentrate on making a life after baseball. Check with me in a few weeks and maybe I'll be able to let you know the details. Now I've got to go back into the dugout. Farrell's trying to save this game for me so I can finish with a win." He turned on his heel and walked back through the door, ignoring the shouted questions of the media.

"He's going back? But he's hurt."

"Hush, Lucille." Dusty's father wiped at his eyes then straightened his shoulders. "You know Dusty. He's a team player, always has been. We'll talk to him after it's over."

Dusty's dad guided them back to the elevator and they rode it in silence. Stevie felt stunned. It was over. Just like that. A career Dusty had spent his whole life building had ended in the blink of an eye.

How would Bebe react to this? Would she still meet

him? If she did, would she punish him for disappointing her or offer her sympathy? Stevie rubbed her aching forehead. Too much, too fast.

When they settled in their seats, the scoreboard blazed with news of Dusty's retirement. He came out on the field to a standing ovation. Fans cheered and cried and cheered until finally he walked out to the pitcher's mound and placed a ball in the new pitcher's hand and waved his cap one more time.

"That boy's a class act," Stevie's father said after they'd all cheered until they were hoarse. Stevie sat through three more innings of baseball, her head throbbing. Dusty loved her. She loved him. She'd be a fool to let a few differences keep them from enjoying whatever time they might have together.

A life, a career, it all could end in an instant at the whims of fate or a hard-hit baseball. Look at Riley. He'd talked about marrying and settling down some day. Then a drug dealer had taken away Riley's somedays with one shot from a handgun.

She worried about how to approach Dusty. She'd rejected him over and over again until his pride was hurt. She had to tell him she loved him, had always loved him and would do whatever it took to make a life with him. Surely he would listen.

After the game, Cap Hawlsey pulled her aside outside the players' dressing rooms.

"Hope this don't set her off," Cap muttered.

Stevie looked to make sure none of the parents were within earshot. "I know. She was so fixated on this record."

"I've got security tight here. But you go home with him and make sure the lady ain't waiting for him. You got backup?"

"Sure." Stevie's stomach plunged and she gripped

her purse, reassured by the hard shape of her gun. Let Bebe try it. Let her come close to Dusty and . . . her mind went blank when he finally emerged. Both his parents hugged him, shedding more tears and fussing over him until he finally pled exhaustion.

"Dusty, I . . ."

"Will you drive me home, Stevie?" He looked grim, his eyes dull. Stevie made the mistake of grabbing his elbow to support him and he jerked away, hissing with pain.

"Don't touch it. I'm close to losing it here. Let's just move out."

"S-sorry." Stevie held open the door, relieved that Cap's security force had cleared out the media.

Mark had the Ferrari at the curb. He murmured words of sympathy and helped Dusty into the passenger seat.

"Mark, I need backup at Dusty's house. Radio the team that we're moving out." Stevie slid into the driver's seat and adjusted it closer to the pedals.

"Will do. Linda and I'll get there as quick as we can. Think you'll need some uniforms?"

"Well—"

"No! I don't want any publicity!" Dusty fastened his seat belt, his face rigid with the effort.

"Okay, I'll handle it. But, Mark, get there as soon as you can." Stevie shut her door and put the car in gear. The car squealed and lurched and Dusty cursed.

"Sorry, this clutch is—"

"Just drive, Stevie. I took a handful of painkillers and I'm about to pass out. Since I'd hate for you to have to drag me into the house, you'd better hurry."

Stevie bit her lip. What had she expected? For Dusty to cry on her shoulder? Naturally he was snapping at her. He was in pain and the last time they'd talked, she'd made it sound as if making love with him was no big deal. Could he ever forgive her?

She concentrated on driving. The car was so powerful it seemed to drive her, but she only killed the engine once at a red light. By the time they arrived at Dusty's gate, he was snoring softly, slumped against the door.

Stevie saw Ranger dancing around in the headlights and an unfamiliar white pickup truck in the driveway.

"Oh, God. Bebe's here."

Twelve

Stevie turned off the engine and looked over her shoulder. Where were the cops she'd expected to pull in behind her? Stevie grabbed Dusty's cell phone and punched in a number. The dispatcher told her a flat tire had delayed the pair of officers assigned to her. Did she need additional backup? Stevie glanced at her watch, mentally calculating how long changing a tire could take. But she wasn't going to repeat her mistakes.

"Yes, send all the backup you can." She ended the call and looked at the house. A light went on in Dusty's bedroom. Dusty was sleeping soundly. Grabbing her gun out of her purse, she pulled the keys from the ignition and locked him in.

Ranger waited for her outside the car, barking frantically and running up to the back door. Stevie quietly opened the door, pushing the dog back to keep him outside. The alarm had been disarmed even though the code had been changed just yesterday. How . . . ? She'd have to figure that out later. Right now she crept across the darkened den, scanning corners, her gun at the ready. To her surprise, her hand shook.

She stopped and told herself to stay calm. Surprise was on her side. Stevie moved toward the hall.

Dusty's bedroom door was ajar, light spilling through the crack. Stevie braced herself and nudged it open with her foot. Dusty's bed was torn apart, the spread slashed, pillows on the floor. And she smelled gasoline. She kept her gun close, and the safety off, but she was terrified. If she had to shoot . . . The room looked empty and Stevie eased inside.

"Oof!" Something slammed into her from behind, hitting her at the back of her knees. She went down but kept her gun in her hand. Another rookie mistake. Always check behind the door. Adrenaline pumped through her and anger. Furious at herself and at Bebe, she tried to roll over but another hard shove pushed her face across the carpet, burning her cheek. A heel jammed into her wrist and she grunted with pain.

"Damned bitch! What are you, a cop?" a husky voice said near her ear. A cloying perfume almost overpowered the gasoline smell and made Stevie's stomach heave. The woman was so damned heavy she couldn't breathe.

"You're under arrest. You have the right—" Stevie bucked, trying to fling Bebe off her back.

"You *are* a cop! I should have known Dusty would never fall for such a—" Bebe grabbed Stevie's hair, yanking until Stevie's eyes watered. The other woman's knee pressed on Stevie's wrist until she felt it go numb, her hand opening in spite of her desperate efforts to keep it closed on her gun.

"Got you now." With a laugh and a final wrench at her scalp, Bebe grabbed the gun and rolled away. "Get up."

Stevie gasped, the agony in her wrist convincing her it might be broken. She crawled to her knees, using her left hand to lever herself to her feet. Finally, she turned to stare at Bebe. The woman—hell, was she a woman?—wore a brassy wig, slightly askew, and carefully applied heavy makeup.

"What now, Bebe?" Stevie held her injured wrist, calculating just what it would take to get her gun back. Bebe held it steady, obviously familiar with firearms. Not an encouraging sign. Bebe glanced in the mirror above Dusty's dresser and straightened her wig. Stevie decided to take a chance, lunging for the gun. Reacting instantly, Bebe whacked Stevie hard on her shoulder with the gun butt.

A new pain for Stevie's collection. She faced Bebe, panting, determined to look for another chance to take her out.

"Behave, lady, or I'll shoot you right now. I probably will anyway, but it would be more fun if we could get Dusty in here to watch." She smiled, her lips a parody in flame red that had been smeared during the struggle.

Blinking back tears of pain, Stevie held her shoulder. "Don't be stupid, Bebe. Backup will be here any minute. Cop killers go to death row. You willing to risk that?"

Bebe paused, the gun finally wavering a bit. "Maybe I'll use you as hostage. You and Dusty. Where is he?"

"He's still in the car, out cold. Didn't you see him get hurt?" Stevie studied Bebe's stance, the way she wobbled in her high heels.

"I saw it. I cried. Such a horrible thing." Bebe gestured for Stevie to move out of the room ahead of her.

"So why are you here? Why are you wrecking Dusty's bedroom? I thought you loved him."

"Shut your mouth. You ruined everything. Moving in here. Distracting him. No wonder he didn't break the record."

"I didn't distract him, you did." Stevie walked slowly into the den, her eyes searching the room for anything she might be able to use for a weapon.

"You trying to give me a reason to kill you?" Bebe shoved the gun against Stevie's spine, making her stagger.

"No. Just wondering why you're mad at me and not him." Where was everyone? She should be hearing sirens any moment or at least see the troops bursting through the back door.

"If you hadn't interfered, he might have come to see—" Her voice broke and she sniffled. "But I *am* mad at him now. He failed me. Just two more strikeouts. And he brought you in here after I promised—"

"Paper promises are cheap, Bebe. I gave him the real thing."

"Shut up, you slut. You don't know anything about it, I was going to—" Bebe nudged her in the back with the gun barrel and Stevie pretended to stumble. Pretend? She felt dizzy with pain. But she had to think.

"Was? Does that mean I can have Dusty now?" Stevie felt the gun twitch against her back. A noise at the window made her wonder if her backup . . . No, it was Ranger, barking frantically and leaping at the glass.

"That damned dog. He never liked me." The gun moved and the glass shattered into a thousand pieces. Stevie rammed her shoulder into Bebe's middle, slamming her to the floor. With her good hand, Stevie wrenched the gun from her, springing up to point it down at Bebe. Thank God she'd practiced shooting with her left hand.

"Dusty's never going to forgive you if you've hurt his dog," Stevie said, thanking God when sirens suddenly became loudly evident. To her relief she also heard barking. She looked hard at Bebe, whose wig had landed on the rug next to her. She was swiping at tears that streaked mascara on her cheeks.

"I know you. You're Benny. Security. No wonder you could enter Dusty's house at will."

"How clever of you to finally figure that out," Benny sneered. "Such a waste. If Dusty had just—"

"Police! Freeze!" Stevie sagged with relief when two uniformed policemen burst into the room. She dropped her gun on command. Mark's arrival and a trip to the car to retrieve her badge put an end to the standoff.

"Wait, I want to talk to Benny." Stevie ignored Mark's demands that she let him call an ambulance. Her wrist was killing her, but it could wait. "What now, Benny?"

Benny was sullen and an almost comical sight in a feminine pantsuit, high heels and close-cropped hair. His makeup was so smeared he was clown material, but Stevie knew better than to crack a smile. An obsessed fan who got past gates was one thing, but Benny was knowledgeable about electronic security—and weapons.

"What's the matter, lady? Still worried about your precious boyfriend?" Bebe looked momentarily defiant, until one of the uniformed policemen barked a warning and his shoulders drooped.

Stevie held her breath. She wanted this over with, wanted to be able to tell Dusty. . . .

"What the hell's going on here?" A bleary-eyed Dusty, supported by Mark and Linda, staggered into the room. Ranger trotted at his heels, his hackles rising and a menacing growl coming from his throat when he saw Bebe/Benny.

"Dusty, how could you quit like that!" Benny shouted, struggling between the two policemen.

"You were so close to the record! I loved you!" His cries of disappointment and outrage continued as he was hustled out of the house. Finally a patrol car door slammed and there was silence.

"Did I just see one of my security guards—one of my *male* security guards—in drag? Did he leave here in handcuffs?" Dusty sank down on the couch, his hand on Ranger's head.

"Bebe was Benny. End of story . . ." Stevie blinked when the room swirled around her. She staggered over to a chair, fighting a sudden return of her nausea and arrows of pain in her wrist and shoulder.

"Stevie!" Dusty's concerned shout was the last thing she heard before she fainted for the first time in her life.

"Congratulations, Stevie."

"Thanks for stopping by." Stevie waved her cast at the cluster of old friends who had been waiting in her new office to wish her well on her first day on the job. Gradually the room emptied and Stevie surveyed her new domain, noting a standard issue desk, a new computer and an impressive stack of files in her in-box. Houston had a huge drug problem and she was the fifth person to head a special task force.

She took a deep breath, fighting down panic. It was too much. She would fail, just as the four preceding commanders had. She rubbed her forehead with her good hand and realized she was sweating.

"Very impressive, Detective Powell."

Stevie looked up to see Dusty, his arm in a sling, filling the doorway.

"You're out of the hospital!"

"So are you!" He moved into the small office and

nodded at one of the two armchairs. "Mind if I sit? I'll admit to still being a bit rocky."

"Sure." He settled in the chair with a sigh, adjusting the sling across his chest before pinning her with those impossibly bright eyes.

"You didn't return my calls, Stephanie Jane."

Stevie straightened her already straight blotter. "I . . . there was no point. Bebe was caught. Job done. Over and out."

"Over and out?" He leaned forward and Stevie made herself meet his gaze. "That's it? Job done? What about us?"

"Us?" Stevie tucked her hands in her lap so Dusty couldn't see them shaking. "You know there's no us, Dusty. Never has been. We had our fling. Now—"

"Now? What's changed since Sunday?" He jumped to his feet, striding around the desk to pin her in her seat with his good hand on her shoulder. "Talk to me."

"Talk? Do you want to go over Benny's confession?" She swallowed and rolled her chair back until his hand slid away. "He's definitely going away for a while. He confessed to vandalism, breaking and entering, stalking you, and assaulting a police officer. I'm afraid you're no longer the love of his life."

"Great!" Dusty sat on a corner of her desk and rubbed absently at his shoulder. "That's over, he's made a plea bargain. Adios, Benny. But us—"

"There is no us. I failed you, Dusty. It's a miracle you weren't killed by the guy. There certainly were enough clues. I should have seen—"

"Are you telling me you blame yourself for what happened?" Dusty stood up and grabbed her chin. "You idiot, how can you possibly be responsible for anything? Bebe, Benny, whatever the hell his name is, is the only person responsible for this."

Stevie jerked away from him. "Stop it! I know what I know. You're a civilian, I don't expect you to understand."

"Oh, I understand, all right." He leaned over until his face was only inches from hers. "I understand that you're looking for reasons to reject me again. Don't bother." He stood up, his body rigid. "If you don't love me, then, don't worry, I'll leave quietly and you can forget you ever saw me again." He stared at her, as if trying to see into her heart. Not even years of training could keep the tears from spilling down her cheeks as she studied his dear, dear face.

"Please, don't go. I love you." She'd said it. His face lit and he reached for her. "But we have to—"

"Hush, Stephanie Jane. Let me hold you for a minute before you start talking this to death." He pulled her up and into his arms. Stevie rested her cheek against his chest, careful to stay on his right side, away from his injured shoulder. She felt so safe, so loved. Tears continued running down her face and she sniffled, then reached for the box of Kleenex in her top drawer.

"I . . . I'm sorry. It's just—"

"I told you to hush, love. Now just stand here and listen for a second."

Stevie wiped her cheeks and blew her nose as quietly as possible. "Okay."

"I want you to marry me, Stephanie Jane. I love you. Maybe even started loving you back at the Three Palms Motor Court."

"You finally got it right." Stevie laughed shakily.

"What? The proposal?"

"No, the name of the motel." Oh, God, it felt so good just to stand here, held close to him, surrounded by love. "But, Dusty—"

"Here it comes." Dusty leaned back and stroked the hair back from her face. "But what?"

"I'm not sure you're being realistic. How can you want to marry me? I'm a working woman, a cop who's spent a lot of years to get where I am. I can't just chuck it all to stay at home and be the 'little woman.' " Her voice quavered and Stevie knew she was about to burst out crying. Most men hated tears and she usually considered them a form of emotional blackmail. They had to discuss this rationally before this marriage talk, as thrilling as it was, continued.

"I'm proud of what you've become. Don't you think I realize how hard you must have worked to be considered good enough to take on the entire city's drug problems?" Dusty tilted her chin. "I want a partner for life, a real wife, not a 'little woman.' You can keep your job, though I won't say I'm sorry you'll do it in an office instead of out on the streets duking it out with the likes of Benny the cross-dressing stalker."

"Your macho image still smarting a bit from that, Mr. Derrick?" Stevie couldn't hold back a watery grin at the look on his face. "Hey, we kept it out of the papers. Be grateful."

"Grateful. Of course. But when I think of you rolling around on the floor, getting your wrist broken—"

"It happens. May happen again if this task force folds and I have to go back out on the streets." Stevie could see him considering that. She hated the thought herself. Her tussle with Bebe/Benny had brought it all back. The fear, the surge of adrenaline and then the letdown. Not to mention the ever-present threat of death. . . .

"We'll cross that bridge when we come to it," he said quietly, pulling her close again. "I'm not lying when I say the possibility scares the hell out of me, but

I can take whatever comes, as long as I know you love me."

"Oh, Dusty. I do love you." Okay, so maybe she was entitled to a tear or two. She'd been through such an emotional wringer lately and now he was being so wonderful.

"I want us to have a family, Stevie. What do you think?"

Stevie realized she'd stiffened. She looked up at him and took a breath. "I'd love to start a family, but my job—"

He smiled and wiped another tear from her cheek. "I'm retired, remember? I can hold off the broadcasting for awhile, or do something part-time. What if you have the babies and I'll stay home and raise them? Of course, with my mother, your mother and Ivy supervising to make sure I don't put diapers on backwards." He leaned down and planted a lingering kiss on her lips that made Stevie want to lock her door and initiate her new office in a very interesting way. Finally, Dusty rested his chin on her hair.

"Marry me soon, Stephanie Jane. We're not getting any younger."

"You've got this all figured out, don't you?" Stevie tried to work up some anger at his high-handedness, but she was just too happy, too thoroughly, deliriously happy. Dusty. Children. Her own identity.

She pulled his face down with her good hand behind his neck and gave him another kiss designed to curl his toes. He growled and pulled her closer with his good hand. Stevie giggled and he raised his head.

"What's so funny?"

"Us. With maybe two good arms between us." Stevie loved the way he looked at her, a combination of love and lust that had her own toes curling.

"You know, it's taken you a long time, Dusty."

"What? My mother's calling this the shortest courtship on record." Dusty grinned. "What is it—a week and a half?"

"Try fifteen years. I've loved you for fifteen years, Mr. Derrick. I'd say you owe me an awful lot of . . ." She leaned close to whisper some suggestions in his ear.

"Whoa! A fella could hurt himself trying to please you." He dug in his pocket and picked up her left hand. He slipped a large diamond engagement ring on her finger. "Your mother gave me your ring size, along with a lecture. I'm going to make an honest woman of you, Stephanie Jane."

Stevie looked down at the sinfully large diamond and then up at the sinfully handsome man who was the love of her life. "You can try, Dusty. You can try."

ABOUT THE AUTHOR

Lynn McKay has been hooked on romance novels since she read *Gone With the Wind* in the seventh grade. She's still sure Scarlett and Rhett lived happily ever after. Lynn loves traveling, gourmet eating and gossip. She lives in Texas with her husband, son and spoiled-rotten lap dog.

Lynn would love to hear from readers at:

P.O. Box 101
League City, TX 77574-0101